Regaining The Unlost

(NOVEL)

R.M.Prabhulinga Shastry

PG PUBLICATION

Delhi - 110089 (India)

Edition : First published in paperback in 2021
ISBN : 978-93-90889-22-8

Regaining The Unlost
By : R.M.Prabhulinga Shastry

Price : 465/-

Cover page & Layout
Jyoti

Published by
Prakhar Goonj Publication
H-3/2, Sector - 18, Rohini, Delhi - 110089
Contact : 7982710571, 7838505899, 011-42635077
Email : prakhargoonj@gmail.com,
sinha.neelu123@gmail.com
web : prakhargoonjpublications.com

Preface

Spiritually "S'HE'" is keeping alertness
To be "S'HE'" from time immemorial.

Mentally "WO'MAN'" has been worshipping
'MAN' to retaining Herness as to be S'HE'.

Physically "FE'MALE'" is being dominated
By 'MALE' but is struggling to be HU'MAN'.

From time immemorial Human being kind is suffering from the bondage which in't visible but understood. Several schools of thoughts have been brought out in this regard to learn what it would be.

Several Theoreticians have sincerely studied the reasons lie behind the bondage. Each and Every Theoretician, undoubtedly has reached such a stage. But not a particular Theoretician has reached the Ultimate stage.

The same thing has been happened in the East and in the West also. But in the East there are the envisioners who had envisioned the Thing. It can be understood that the Thing which is envisioned couldn't be defined but can be understood that Thing only exists from Beginningless to Endlessness. This Thing, which couldn't be defined as the Matter or The Energy or The Subject would be many as well as One. It is strange to note that this One is not actually a number or a figure. It might be addressed as Zero. From this Zero only all which, exist and continue, merge in that Zero. It is very strange to note that all which are in existence are not separated from Zero. This Zero has been envisioned by the Indians, has been studied by the Indians is being preached by the Indians who have ultimately reached the reason which reveals what is the bondage and how to get emancipated from that bondage. This is the Indian thought which has been debated by a Female Human being and a Male human being to get free from 'Human', 'Male', 'Female' and 'ing' ultimately to be as 'BE' which stands for Zero.

R.M.Prabhulinga Shastry
H.No: 3-132, Balajinagar,
Mahabubnagar,
Telangana State – India
PIN: 509001.
Mobile No: 9441628134
8309367653
Email Id:rmprabhulingashastry@gmail.com

Index

Chapter-1

"Isn't it wrong with You?"

"What is wrong with me?"

"Your amorous looking at me."

"I don't feel it is wrong."

"But I don't accept Your such looking. So I treat that it is wrong with You."

"Why don't You accept mine?"

"Why should I do as You desire?"

"I am for doing so whereas You are for receiving so."

"Doing so may be Your choice but receiving so is mine."

"So only I demand You to receive mine."

"I mean receiving so is mine is that it is my choice I may receive or may not."

"I am demanding You receive and behave accordingly."

"I am too demanding You not to demand me to receive Yours."

"Why are You doing such demand?"

"Why are You doing alike?"

"Amn't I to do so?"

"No, You aren't to do"

"Without me, how can You meet Your urge?"

"Without me, can You do Your own?"

"So only, I am doing."

"But I am not getting such feeling at the moment."

"In the next moment, when You get so, do You receive?"

"Whenever I get so, I wouldn't receive Yours."

"Why? What wrong is with me?"

"It is absolutely my option to whom I ought to credit."

"Would that, whom You credit to, differ from me?"

"Couldn't You learn there is a lot of difference between You and any one who is like You."

"Pertaining to the matter no one who is like me is ever same as how I am but to the subject, could You find any difference between any one who is like me and myself?"

"As far as concerned to the subject, could You find any difference between You, who are not like how I am in the matter, and me?"

"To the subject, none could find any difference between any two. But both You and I are now with the matter of which our bodies made."

"So,"

"So only, I am to demand You and You are to receive."

"Is there no other to demand like me?"

"Is there no other like You to receive like You to whom I am demanding?"

"Don't You know?"

"I know. But I am demanding only You not some other who is like You."

"Why are You doing me only."

"I couldn't tell why I am doing You only."

"I too couldn't tell why I am not receiving Yours."

"You know as what I am I can do so. At the same time as what You are You can receive. Can't You?"

"Yes. I know."

"Then, why can't You?"

"I can't answer You."

"Why? Are You unable to answer my question?"

"This is not question of ability and inability."

"Then What?"

"The reason I don't have reason or I might have lost the reason."

"When You have lost the reason, wouldn't I have too lost the reason?"

"When we, all the bits_of only I, have put on the bodies of matter, We have simultaneously lost the reason of the State of all of us."

"When we, all the bits_of only I have lost the reason as You said, what will be wrong with You if You receive me?"

"Though we, all the bits of only I, have lost the reason, we ought to be rationalistic."

"Rationalistic!"

Chapter-2

"Yes. Rationalistic"

"What is Rationalism?"

"Rationalism means the Practice of treating reason as the ultimate authority."

"Here once again You say 'reason'. Without learning what is 'reason', how can You or I treat it the ultimate authority?"

"Before learning 'reason' we have to know and learn the Practice."

"The Practice!"

"Yes. The Practice."

"What does Practice mean?"

"The Practice imports three meanings. They are
1) Doing of Something,
2) Way of Doing and
3) Systematic repetition."

"Yes. As You said, I am doing something."

"What are You doing?"

"I am looking at You; it is my doing something. I am amorously looking at You; it is my way of doing and I am again and again looking at You amorously, it is my systematic repetition."

"Before looking at me, did You suppose that You had to look at me?"

"No, I didn't suppose."

"Without supposing, how are You doing?"

"How am I?"

"So, Your doing is not at all doing?"

"You mean doing must need supposition."

"Yes. Doing supposition is indispensable."

"Why does Doing need supposition?"

"Because, Supposition gradually gets translated into thinking."

"Thinking !"

"Yes. Thinking, But at first You have to suppose that 'I have to look'. This supposition makes think and think."

"Then!"

"This thinking gradually is directed."

"Who or Which directs the thinking?"

"The Will."

"Will ?"

"Yes. The Will."

"What is the Will ?"

" 'Will' means mental power by which one can direct one's thoughts and actions and does influence those of others."

"What is mental?"

"Mental means of or in the Mind."

"What does the Mind mean?"

"The Mind means that which animates the body and is distinct from it."

"Isn't the Mind a part or an organ of body?"

"The body is also comprised of the Mind. But this Mind isn't an organ of the body and it is ever distinct from the body."

"Isn't the Mind the Atman (the Soul)?"

"Don't You know it? As the Subject, both we are the Atman (the Soul) which is indivisible between all (us) but both we are separated from each other."

"When You say the Mind is distinct from the body, isn't it the Atman (the Soul) ?"

"No, never. The Mind is with the body into which the Atman(the Soul) enters, so, though the Mind can be seemed or assumed as the Atman(the Soul), it couldn't be the Atman (the Soul) which is always beyond the body made of five elements into which it enters."

"Then, What does the Mind do?"

"The Mind would animate the body, This animating of the Mind is only the Mental Power."

"What is the use of Mental Power?"

"By this Mental Power One can direct One's thoughts and actions and influence those of others."

"Who is the One?"

"This One is that One Who is the indweller in the body but not the Atman (the Soul)."

"How can this One be?"

"As long as the Atman (the Soul) goes on as the indweller in the body, that Atman (the Soul) though it is beyond the body, would be the One."

"Aren't both the Atman (the Soul) and the One one and the same."

"No doubt at all both the Atman (the Soul) and One are one and the same."

"Then, What is difference between the Atman (the Soul) and this One?"

"Macro-form of the_Atman (the Soul) is the Mind and the Micro-form of Mind is the Atman (the Soul). When the Atman (the Soul) enters into the body made of five elements while keeping Itself beyond five elements, in Its Macro-form It would go on as the One who as the One would get attached with One's own associations consequent to One's own activities done as the indweller in the body of five elements."

"Why would this One be got attached with One's own association(s)?"

"Because each and every One's activity contains the Mind, the Word and the Action."

"So what?"

"The first is the Mind which could only direct one's thoughts. When this One applies One's Mind properly, these directed-thought or thoughts become one's 'Will'."

"What is the necessity for the thoughts to be 'Will'?"

"Then only, Your looking would be at will."

"At will! Must every doing be at will ?"

"Yes. Every doing must be at will."

"Why?"

"That, which is done at will, could be in favour of one who does 'doing' as a part of 'Will'?"

Chapter-3

"When would the doing be at will?"

"When the Mind would function properly, the doing would be at will?"

"How can the Mind function properly?"

"The Mind could itself decide whether its functioning is proper or not."

"On what basis it could decide?"

"Itself is the base for its deciding."

"At present, is Your Mind functioning properly?"

"Yes, My Mind is functioning properly."

"How can You tell?"

"So only, I am not receiving You."

"You mean my demanding is not proper."

"There You are."

"How can You say I am not doing properly?"

"How could You have looked at me amorously ?"

"Because, I am to look at You. Amn't I?"

"Yes, You are."

"Then! What wrong is with me?"

"You can look at me but You shouldn't do so amorously."

"Actually I have not prepared even to look at You. But I have done to do so amorously."

"To be prepared is only the Supposition."

"Why have I to suppose?"

"When You suppose whether You should do something or something else, then, You can be let prepared to suppose."

"Why should I prepare?"

"Because Your preparation reflects not only Yourself but others too."

"What will happen if others are reflected?"

"Why should others be made to be reflected by Your doing? Those, who are reflected, would fall down from their dignity or get to be far off from their disposition."

"What is the dignity ?"

"The dignity is such level of the state at which one has overpowered the influence of bodily senses."

"What would be wrong with those who would fall down or get to be far-off?"

"They would replace You."

"You mean?"

"They will too do what You are now doing?"

"Let them do."

"When they are got reflected, they would do like You even they might do more than what You are now doing. Thus they would be accountable for those who would get reflected by them."

"Accountable!"

"Yes. Accountable!"

"When, at first, I might have got them reflected before they would get some others reflected, then, am I too accountable?"

"Certainly, The first-one will be You only to be accountable."

"If I will have been accountable, what would happen to me?"

"You will have to go on as 'You' in this 'World' which has just come into existence when The Only "I" would have been but there would have not been 'You and I', have done 'Will' to be 'Many'."

"World!"

Chapter-4

"Can't You remember when both You and I have talked to each other while something was happening to us?"

"No, I can't remember. Can You remember so? If You can, please reproduce it that must be verbatim."

"Ok. Now You can listen Yourself to same conversation had between You and me."

"What is happening to us?"

"Both we are gradually losing our Omnipotence, Omniscience and Omnipresence."

"Is this really happening?"

"No, It is not. But it is our Illusion which we cherish that we are not Omnipotent, Omniscient and Omnipresent."

"What would happen from it?"

"Then, we couldn't do like Omnipotent, Omniscient and Omnipresent."

"If we suppose to do like Omnipotent, Omniscient and Omnipresent, then couldn't we do like Omnipotent, Omniscient and Omnipresent?'

"No, We couldn't do at all."

"Why?"

"As we have already cherished the Illusion, now we are immersing in the Illusion."

"Can't we ourselves desist from immersing in the Illusion and come out from it?"

"We can't now."

"Why?"

"As per cherishing of Illusion, each and every 'I' would go down upto that level or that range which each and every 'I' have cherished."

"In the middle of immersing of each and every 'I', couldn't each and every 'I' get to desist oneself from immersing ?"

"Couldn't."

"Why?"

"Because, there is no span of time between cherishing Illusion and immersing in it."

"It means?"

"It means, cherishing and immersing would happen simultaneously."

"How?"

"Because, there is no difference between cherishing and

immersing. Cherishing the Illusion means nothing but immersing in it."

"Would the level or the range differ from one another ?"

"Certainly and indubitably. There is no same level or range in cherishing or immersing in Illusion between any two of each and every 'I'."

"What would be the aftermath of such difference between any two?"

"Each and every 'I' would differ from any another one of each and every 'I' in one item or many items of the quality or qualities."

"Are there Many qualities in each and every 'I'?"

"Yes. There are. The Only "I" would do 'Will' to be 'Many' in both Subject and Matter and at the same time the Matter to be 'Many' in the qualities."

"Regarding the Subject?"

"The Subject is one and the same."

"Then, Why do One each and every 'I' differ in quality from any Another one of each and every 'I'?"

"Because, the level or the range of cherishing or immersing in the Illusion of each and every 'I' would result in so."

"When the Subject wouldn't differ, how does the Matter affect each and every 'I'?"

"Actually the Matter wouldn't affect any one of each and every 'I'. But the cherishing or the immersing of each and every 'I' in the Illusion would affect the item or the items of any one or many of the quality or the qualities."

"How is it?"

"According to cherishing or immersing of each and every 'I' in the Illusion, each and every 'I' would enter into the body comprised of the Many."

"Of which, the Many comprised?"

"Of five elements. They are The Space, The Air, The Fire, The Water and The Earth."

"Is there any relation between or among these elements?"

"In fact and in truth all are one. In the 'Many' only i.e. when The Only "I" do 'Will' to be 'Many' 'only, they would differ from one another."

"What is the difference between or among them?"

"They are three in the kind. The Space is the first element. It is not like The Air, The Water or The Earth which contains so many ingredients each of which has its own kind and even it is not like The Fire which is not like The Air, The Water or The Earth containing of its own ingredients of its own kind."

"Does the Fire go on as one and the same without getting into any changes?"

"The Fire, in truth, is one and the same as it wouldn't increase or decrease and it gets end or destruction etc., but it would get into so many forms."

"Forms! What are they?"

"They are no other things of The Fire. All they are the Fire only. Each form of the Fire would seem as peculiar in its kind do or behave peculiarly as per its kindness."

"Does any form of the Fire do or behave like another form of the Fire?"

"Doesn't. Doing or behaving of each and every form of the Fire would differ from another each and every form of the Fire."

"Like form of the Fire, would The Air, The Water and The Earth or any other ingredient of any of The Air, The Water or The Earth do or behave?"

"No, none of either The Air, The Water or The Earth or any ingredient of The Air, The Water or The Earth could do or would do."

"When there are differences among the five elements, is there any relation between any two of elements or among all elements?"

"Yes. There is relation among them."

"What is it?"

"From The Space, The Air would take birth or come out in The Space, from The Air The Fire, from The Fire The Water and from The Water The Earth."

"When remaining all four elements take birth or come out directly or indirectly from The Space only, then, Why are they called as elements?"

"They are not only elements but basic-elements or fundamental elements also. These basic or fundamental elements would contain or become other elements."

"Why do these basic or fundamental elements would contain or become other elements?

"For various kinds of matter and various kinds of bodies into which each and every 'I' would enter in different ratios, off-springs of basic or fundamental elements would be made of basic or fundamental elements. Thus they would contain or become elements."

"Is no body there, in which each and every 'I' am or any item of other matter than any body in which each and every 'I' am, beyond these basic or fundamental elements?"

"No, either this body or any item of matter is not beyond the World i.e. basic or fundamental elements."

"What is the World?"

"The World is the Creation which contains five basic or fundamental elements. These basic or fundamental elements would be called as Water, Orb, Room, Light and Draught. So, The WORLD is an acronym of these descriptive terms of five basic or fundamental elements."

"Does the entire World comprise of each and every 'I'?

"No, the Entire World doesn't comprise of each and every 'I'. Each and Every 'I' would enter into the body comprised of the matter i.e. basic or fundamental elements."

"When each and every 'I' would enter into the body comprised of the matter i.e. basic or fundamental elements, isn't the World a combination in which each and every 'I' am a thing or each and every 'I' amn't a component of the World or isn't the World a compound that contains each and every 'I'?"

"No, The World isn't a combination, a mixture that contains each and every 'I' as one of components and a compound." "Without any relation with the World, do each and every 'I' enter into the body comprised of the World?"

"Yes. Without having any materialistic relation with the world, each and every 'I' would enter into the World."

"How?"

"That is the Illusion which each and every 'I' do cherish."

"Actually the Illusion is what ?"

"It is not something or someone beyond each and every 'I'. When The Only "I" do 'Will' to be 'Many' as the Matter and the Subject i.e. each and every 'I', then each and every 'I' would cherish the Illusion that each and every 'I' am not the Omnipresent but the limited, not the Omniscient but the little-knower and not the Omnipotent but the little-potent."

"By cherishing the Illusion, what would happen to each and every 'I'?"

"Having been done so, each and every 'I' would enter into the body comprised of the Matter. Thus each and every 'I' would be limited to be within that body in which each and every 'I' would have entered."

"So what?"

"Having been limited alike, each and every 'I' would have been a being from then."

"A being! What is it?"

"When each and every 'I' would enter into a body comprised of basic or fundamental elements, from then, that body would become potent to be active to do will any, some or everything or do any, some or everything."

"Then, do each and every 'I' do like The Only "I"?"

"Each and every 'I' can do like The Only "I". But owing to have cherished the Illusion, that each and every 'I' can't do like The Only "I", each and every 'I' wouldn't do everything but do one or some."

"When each and every 'I' can do one or few things, can each

and every 'I' have the knowledge?"

"Each and every 'I' am myself the knowledge actually. But doing cherishing the Illusion, each and every 'I' would be myself limited to have known as little-knower."

"Now I am sure You have learnt that each and every 'I' i.e. either You or I would do one or some as little-knowers."

"Yes, I can have done. As a little-knower, can't 'I' look at You?"

"You can. But You ignore that You are little-knower."

"So What!"

"As a little-knower You can suppose the thing at least in its least quantity."

"How?"

"Because, little-knower doesn't mean absolute unknower of anything, instead knower of at least one thing which can be very little-thing that might not be taken into consideration. The knower of that little thing can suppose before doing something."

"How can You have come to conclusion that I have not supposed?"

"Tell me first of all, have You supposed before looking at me?"

"You are correct. I have not done. But I would like to know how You have done?"

"If You have supposed, You would have looked at me decently but not amorously."

"Doesn't looking at You decently need supposition?"

"It does too need."

"What is difference between doing supposition for look at decently and look at amorously?"

"There can be a lot of scope that decency would keep another be decent whereas amorousness may or might or can affect decency of another."

"Can't another keep its own decency without being affected?"

"Many a time can't."

"Why?"

"Another is also like You who have cherished the Illusion and are going on as one of each and every 'I'."

"It may be so. But why can't It keep its own?"

"Any One, who has cherished the Illusion and entered into the body of the Matter comprised of five elements, is not at all like The Only "I" all in all. Therefore, none of each and every 'I' could judge or adjudge oneself (myself) whether one shall receive looking at amorously."

"If someone of each and every 'I' could judge or adjudge oneself as one shall receive looking at amorously, then ?"

"Then, for that someone of each and every 'I' who could judge or adjudge oneself as one shall receive so, that looking at amorously would not be amorously but decently."

"How?"

"When judgement or adjudgement is not with misfeasance, then, the receiver-one couldn't be affected."

"The receiver-one might not be affected. But the amorousness couldn't be the decency. Could it?

"When the receiver-one couldn't be affected at all, then, both the receiver-one and the doer-one would be in same level or range ."

"So What?"

"Any two, who are in the same level or range in any item, in that item they are not separated from each other. Instead they are only 'One'. To achieve this Oneness in each and every item is for each and every 'I'."

Chapter-5

"What are levels and ranges? What has happened or would happen from these?"

"In consequent of cherishing the Illusion, though both You and I are The Only "I" only, we have been each and every 'I' as if separated from The Only "I" and separated from each other."

"Since when we have been?"

"Since both You and I have cherished the Illusion."

"In which we have been as if separated?"

"You ought to know and learn that since then not only both You and I, one each and every 'I' would sexually differ from another each and every 'I' also."

"What is this sexual difference arisen between one each and every 'I' and another each and every 'I'?"

"If You don't remember, recollect Your memory that each and every 'I' would cherish the Illusion in certain level or range."

"Yes. I recollect."

"The level or the range of cherishing the Illusion would also be in Being and Doing of each and every 'I'."

"What are 'Being and Doing'?"

"To be as The Only "I" am and to do as The Only "I" do."

"Oh! Is there also the level or the range in these Being and Doing?"

"Yes."

"Is it only in Being or Doing only?"

"No, it is in both."

"Why is it so?"

"Because, The Only "I" would be The Only "I" forever while doing one, some or everything. Even doing nothing of The Only "I" would ever be a doing."

"Is the level or the range of cherishing the Illusion same in being and doing?"

"The difference of the level or the range of cherishing of Illusion in being and doing is only the sexual difference between one each and every 'I' and another each and every 'I'."

"What is the sexual difference?"

"Sexual difference would divide the beings into two."

"What are they?"

"One being is male and another being is female."

"Why does one being become male and another one female?"

"The level or the range of cherishing the Illusion in Being of each and every 'I' is less than in Doing of each and every 'I', then, that each and every 'I' would be male-being. If the level or the range of cherishing is vice-versa, then, that each and every 'I' would be female-being."

"Did all of each and every 'I' who have become male- beings cherish the Illusion same level or range in Being less than the Doing?"

"No, All of each and every 'I' didn't. One of each and every 'I' who have become male-being did not cherish the Illusion in Being at same level or range of another one of each and every 'I' who have become male-being."

"So, isn't each and every male being same?"

"Yes, even each and every female-being isn't also same."

"Aren't any two of male-beings same?"

"In Which?"

"Level or range of cherishing in being less than doing."

"No, each and every male-being would have its own level or range."

"Regarding female-beings?"

"Same alike male-beings."

"Is the level or the range of cherishing the Illusion of each and every 'I' who would be male-being equal in that of each and every 'I' who would be female-being?"

"Yes, there would be one or some male-beings that would equal in one or some female-beings in their and their levels and ranges in cherishing the Illusion in being and doing."

"Could such male-being which has such level or range know and learn such female being which has same such level or range?"

"It could."

"Then, what is the Problem?"

"The Problem is to have been under the impact of cherishing the Illusion."

"How long would that impact go on existing ?"

"Forever."

"How could it be receded or vanished?"

"It would never recede or vanish itself."

"Then, who could expunge it?"

"One Oneself could do so."

"One could Oneself ! Who is that One?"

"That One is each and every male-being and female-being ."

"Could male-being itself expunge its impact of cherishing ? At the same time, could female-being itself do so?"

"Yes, male-being and female-being do so separately or individually and at the same time could do so jointly or co-operating with each other or without knowledge of both or any one of both."

"Does that expunging of the impact of the Illusion cherished go on gradually or complete at a time?"

"It would go on neither gradually nor complete at a time."

"Then, how is it done?"

"The expunging would either go on or fluctuate."

"Again and again, would each and every 'I' be affected by the impact of cherishing the Illusion or would each and every 'I' cherish the Illusion again and again?"

"Scope would be there for both."

"When would each and every 'I' be affected again and again and when would each and every 'I' cherish the Illusion again and again?"

"In course of expunging the impact of cherishing, either male-being or female-being couldn't know and learn what is actually the Illusion and cherishing it. Though it couldn't do so and so, without its own knowledge it would strive and struggle to get away from that impact of the Illusion cherished or directly from that Illusion cherished. As it would go on while striving and struggling without having any kind of capacity to know and learn, it would get through a stage at which it would have the knowledge which would have to be manifested by itself. From this stage, it would persist its striving and struggling to manifest the knowledge which is actually in it in the form of each and every 'I'. This manifestation is only the Education. To educate is to know and keep that knowing to be exerted or exercised by the being for the being at least to withstand what it would be at the time at which it would be better than what it was when it wasn't able to notice what it was when it wasn't able to notice what was itself. If this keeping of that knowing would go on incessantly, then, that being would retain its state at which its Illusion would have receded. If this being fails, ignores or neglects its keeping of this knowing for the period of the least span of time, then, it would be affected by itself or without its knowledge it would cherish once again the Illusion actually without knowing or learning what is the Illusion.

Chapter-6

"Are You sure that because of 'Being and Doing' of The Only "I", one of each and every 'I' and another one of each and every 'I' would differ in sex as the male and the female."

"Yes. I am sure."

"Do these 'Being and Doing' of The Only "I" have their own existence either beyond The Only "I" or in, within or with The Only "I"?"

"No, they don't have existence at all. They didn't have or wouldn't have also ever."

"Are they outcomes of the 'Will' done by The Only "I"?"

"No, they aren't either outcomes of The 'Will' done by The Only "I" or the characters of The Only "I"."

"Then, what are they?"

"Before the 'Will' done by The Only "I", "I" without preceded by 'Only' and 'The' and even without followed by any form of 'Be' i.e. am, or was even Be—itself, would be there."

"You mean "I" !"

"Yes. "I","I","I"......."

"Then, what are Be and Do?"

"When "I", who was without preceded by any and without

followed by any, was there that kind of "I" have done 'Will' to be 'Many'. Before doing 'Will' and starting point of doing 'Will', there was a span of time which was the least of the least. This span of time could be termed as the Present. Actually The Only "I" would never have the present, the Past or the Future."

"How?"

"That "I", who never be preceded or followed by any, would have been going on forever and forevermore without having either the beginningness or the endlessness for going on."

"So, wouldn't that "I" have either beginningness or endlessness?"

"Yes, You are correct."

"When that "I" wouldn't have endlessness or beginningness for going on, how does the question of 'Be' arise?"

"The least of the least span, during which, the 'Will' done, would be the Present, Before the Present the period in which The Only "I" went on was the Past and from the starting of the 'Will' done would be the Future."

"Then how would the 'Be' be basic form for the 'Am' and the 'Was'?"

"After the 'Will' done by The Only "I", The Only "I" would have some things which would also be The Only "I". Until The Only "I" do 'Will', there would be no question of any thing even that would also be The Only "I". So, the outcomes of doing 'Will', though they are either true or untrue in existence, are the Future of The Only "I"."

"What are the outcomes?"

"They are 'WILL'."

" 'WILL'! Isn't 'WILL' a single word?"

"No, it is an acronym of Worship, Image, Language and Law."

"Would "I" worship whom?"

"Only The "I" as there would be no some other else than The "I".

"Who would be The "I"?"

"Each and every 'I' would be The "I" and The "I" would be each and every 'I'."

"So, worshipping The "I" would mean worshipping each and every 'I' and worshipping of each and every 'I' to each and every 'I' would mean to worship The "I" only?"

"Yes. there You are."

"Would The "I" have Image of whom ?"

"Only of The Only "I" as there would not be some other or something else than "I". (The Only "I")

"When there would be The Only "I" only, how could The Only "I" be the image?"

"Until The Only "I" do 'Will' "I" was as 'Zero' i.e. there was no one to address "I" i.e. The Only "I" as "I" and "I" would have not too addressed Only "I" as "I". After Only "I" did 'Will', Only "I" or The Only "I" am being addressed by each and every 'I' as "I". This addressing only image."

"Which would be Language of The Only "I"?"

"Only The "I" would be Language as there would be no letters or words or some others to express something as there would not be some or any thing other than The Only "I" and The Only "I" would only be the everything."

"What is the Word?"

"'I' would like to tell You about 'Word' in a poem. Listen to poem.

It must have the meaning
Which can be as an idea
Could be understood and
Would wrap one up in toto.

That, which is an idea,
wouldn't be mingled with
One but strike that one as
Its choice but not at that
Hour when one is in need.

That, which is understood
To one, would be ever with
One but spontaneously isn't
Struck one after some attempt
Must be done as What it is for.

That, which wraps one up in
Toto, would replace one at all
Times so that one ventilates
Anything at anywhere at any
Time without bashfulness.

So only One did not Know and
Has not learnt the Word but is
Observing the Practice to be as
That One who could envision
The Word which 'It'self am "I"
Who am Only the single Word
Which hasn't any at any sides.

"During the existence of 'Will' of The Only "I", would be there one language comprised of its words or many languages?"

"During the existence of 'Will' of The Only "I" or the non-existence of 'Will' of The Only "I", Only "I" would be as One i.e. Singular in kind but all things and beings must have been in Plural in kind. So, the languages would be there while 'Will' of The Only "I" do exist.

"At present in which language, both we are having conversation."

"In English."

"Why are we both doing so in English only?"

"'I' would like to tell this too in a poem. Listen to me."
'E'ducation is manifestation of perfection existing in the human being already.

'N'othing could be remained as existence ultimately.
'G'rammar is made as the policy for things to be let in order

like universes.

'L'etter innovates "I" as the letters that establish the letter is indestructible.

'I' ought to have been learnt as The Only "I" would be there ever.

'S'elf is the subject that could stand for The only "I".

'H'our is certainly conceived as the Illusion at any cost indubitably."

"What would be the Law and who would be the maker of It?"

"Only The "I" would be the Law and its Maker as there would be nothing to be made or enacted and there would be no other to make or enact It on The Only "I".

"How would this or these will be Future of The Only "I".

"Along with this or these 'WILL', The Only "I" would also be there. Actually The Only "I" would go on as The Only "I" beyond 'WILL'."

"So, there are The "I" and the 'WILL' of The Only "I"."

"No, there am The "I" and the 'WILL' of The Only "I"."

"How?"

"Because both The "I" and the 'WILL' of The Only "I" am One and the Same."

"How ?"

"One's' 'Will' couldn't withstand separately from One. The 'WILL' of The Only "I" also wouldn't be there in separation from The "I"."

"When both The "I" and the 'WILL' of The Only "I" am one and the same, why would "I" be followed by Be?"

"After the 'Will' done, since the very beginning of The 'Will', there would be 'I Will' without having any conjection between "I" and 'Will'. Even though the identity of 'Will' seemed, it wouldn't be separate from The "I" besides both "I" and 'Will' am one and the same. To bring out identity of 'WILL' of The Only "I" 'Be' would follow The "I" while indicating the Future of The Only "I".

"So What?"

"When The Only "I" wouldn't be followed by any, The Only "I" would start to be followed at first by 'Be'. So, 'Be' would be the basic form for Am which would indicate the Present and Was which would indicate the Past."

"By indicating Future, Present or Past, what would be revealed by Be or forms of It?"

"The 'Be' and Its forms would reveal the Truthness and Existence of The Only "I"."
"The Truthness and Existence!"

"Yes. By this Truthness and Existence only, The Only "I" wouldn't be followed by the 'Be' or Its forms."

"So,"

"So, The Truth that only would exist forever without having beginningness or endlessness and depend upon only 'Self' would only be The "I" only. So going on of The "I" would ever be nothing but real existing of The "I" as The Truth."

"What would be the existing?"

"Existing would mean to have been being."

"So,"

"So, The "I" would have only been being as The "I" forever."

"The beings wouldn't have been being ever?"

"All the beings would also have been being so. But they have cherished that they would have not been doing so without having beginningness and endlessness as they wouldn't be The "I" only."

"Would they also have been being from time immemorial?"

"They are not they but only The Only "I". For their 'being' from time immemorial, they would be termed as the 'Beings'.

"When they are themselves the 'Beings' and they are being from time immemorial, why would they cherish the Illusion that they would not have been being without having beginningness and endlessness for their 'being'?"

"When The Only "I" do 'WILL', they would cherish the

Illusion that they are being from time i.e. from the beginning of the 'WILL'.

"What is Time?"

"The Time would not be the Absolute Truth like The Only "I". But the Time would be the Truth and even the Untruth like the 'Many' resultant of doing 'WILL' of The Only "I". Before the Present during which The Only "I" would do 'WILL', there was The Only "I". No Time could exist there or No Time would be there. When there was The Only "I", whether there were all of each and every 'I' or not, no any Present each and every 'I' could know learn at all. If they were there, during the Past, whether all of them were those who are at present or not couldn't be known or learnt. It would also not possible for them to know whether all of them in the past i.e. during that Period which was before the Present had been in existence or some of them only had been in so as each and every 'I' or no any each and every 'I' had been in so. So only It could be told as they are being from time immemorial. It means both the Point of Time and the duration of Time couldn't be known and learnt."

"My question is that exactly what is the Time?"

"That, which needs be, do and have

Must perish, end or extinct.
Except only "I" even Time too is That."

"Was or wasn't or were or weren't each and every 'I' in the Past?"

"Some or Many were there."

"In Existence?"

"Yes. But without having identity of them."

"When they had been in Existence, how would they be without their identity?"

"They had been in The Only "I" who would not be preceded or followed by any even by 'The' also. But they couldn't be noticed as existing in that "I". No demarcation was then possible between "I" and them. So, there was no identification of them for any one of each and every 'I', some of each and every 'I' or all of each and every 'I'."

"Why couldn't they know and learn whether they had been in Existence during the Past?"

"Because, they would have cherished that they would not have been The Only "I" but they had been separated from The Only "I" and they had been in existence separately and had separate identity from Only The Only "I"."

"In such state, what would happen to them?"

"When they would cherish the Illusion that they would have come into existence or they would have been in existence from such point of time though they couldn't know and learn that such point of time, their beingness would be cherished as it would have a starting point. By dint of this starting point only the level or the range of beingness of each and every 'I' would be assumed."

Chapter-7

"What is the Truth?"

"Truth is that which could withstand itself as itself forever i.e. eternal without being subject to any. It would have two main qualities. One of them is it could last forever i.e. eternal without having beginningness and endlessness and another one is it would depend only upon itself."

"So, Lasting and Independency are the qualities of the Truth?"

"Yes."

"Then, What or Who is the Truth?"

"Only The Only "I"."

"Is the Truth an adjective of The Only "I"?"

"No, it is not. The Only "I" would ever beyond all adjectives. The Only "I" wouldn't need any adjectives to be qualified. Because each and every adjective would ever be The Only "I" for, of and from The Only "I" only."

"Then, what is the Truth and who am The Only "I"?"

"Both would ever be The Only "I"."

"Then, why would be necessity of the word, the Truth ?"

"To indicate or express the first basic quality of The Only "I"."

"The first basic quality?"

"Yes."

"What is it?"

"Lasting forever without depending upon anything or anybody. Because of this quality The Only "I" would go on as The Only "I" and The Only"I" wouldn't need help of anything or anybody like the verb 'Be' and its other simple-form s."

"Like the 'Be'.....? How?"

"The basic-verb 'Be' for its simple-forms i.e. Am and Was doesn't need any auxiliary for other contractions."

"Would 'Be' be in equal to The Only "I"?"

"In the language, the first basic verb is 'Be' which reveals the existence of the Subject. After the 'Be' only, all other verbs could exist. So, the verb 'Be' is ever independent. Except the verb 'Be', for their simple forms and remaining all other verbs would ever depend upon some other in all other contractions. Like the 'Be' which reveals the existence of the Subject and doesn't depend upon any other, The Only "I" would also never depend upon any other. Whereas the 'Be' would reveal the Subject but The Only "I" would ever be the Subject only. When the existence of the Subject would be revealed by the 'Be' and The Only "I" would only be the Subject, then, the 'Be' would stand for The Only "I" as The Only "I" would never be expressed by any other but only The Only "I" would reveal The Only "I". So 'Be' would be The Only "I" and Thc Only "I" would be the 'Be'."

"Except the 'Be' for its simple forms, would each and every verb need another verb for its other contractions in its simple-forms?"

"Yes. Except 'Do'."

" 'Do?' Then, Do would also be independent like the 'Be'?"

"No, it(Do) would depend upon it(Do) only but not itself."
"How would it be that ?"

"First I would like to tell about do in poetry.
Listen to me.

In each and every basic verb
'Do' would be there.

Do enforces each verb
To express what it sounds.

Do never differs from the verb
In its very or original meaning.

Do also never loses or looses
Its own when it helps another.

Though Do be in the verb to do
It would have its own existence.

Actually Do only would be the base
To all basic verbs being exerted.

The Only "I" would be the Existence
From Beginningless to Endlessness.

The Only "I" only 'do' 'WILL' either
To be 'Many' or not to be 'Many'.

So, in both the Do would be there.
Even 'WILL' would be too the verb.

Hence along with The Only "I" and 'WILL'
Do would seem as in the Existence.

But Do would be emerged at first
When The Only "I" 'WILL', unless couldn't.

'WILL' would as well be in effect
When The Only "I" 'Do', unless couldn't.

Though both 'Do' and 'WILL' would be
Like The Only "I", unlike emerge and merge.

The Only "I" would never emerge or merge
But The Only "I" would be the Cause for them and theirs.

"So, As main verb, 'Do' would need 'Do' as an auxiliary verb for its other contractions. Thus 'Do' would act as the main verb and the auxiliary verb for other contractions to help the main verb 'Do' in other contractions in simple tenses."

"So, there is difference between 'Be' and 'Do' when, 'Do' is differed from the 'Be' in qualities, why would 'Do' be compared with the Be?"

"Because, for both simple present and simple past, both the 'Be' and the 'Do' are same but the 'Be' for its other contractions of simple tenses doesn't need another 'be' as auxiliary verb but 'Do' needs another 'do'.

"Aren't 'Do' as a main verb and as an auxiliary one and the same?"

"In form it would be same but in character they wouldn't be one."

"So, this is the difference between the 'Be' and the 'Do'. Then, how would 'do' differ from other verbs?"

"All other verbs in basic form would need 'do' as an auxiliary. They couldn't and wouldn't act themselves as auxiliaries to themselves."

"So, there is a comparison between the 'Be' and the 'Do'?"

"This is not only a comparison but it would be the second basic quality of The Only "I"."

"The second basic quality ?"

"Yes. When The Only "I" would last forever and depend upon only The Only "I", then, The Only "I" would not go on without doing anything."

"What ! What do The Only "I" do?"

"The Only "I" do 'Will'."

"So, Doing 'Will' is doing of The Only "I"?"

"Yes."

"Then, 'Do' depends upon whom?"

"Upon The Only "I". Doer of 'Will' would be The Only "I"."

"Would 'Do' and The Only "I" differ from each other?"

"No, Both would be one and the same. Owing to doing 'Will' only, 'do' could exist. Besides, The Only "I" would ever be conscious of what The Only "I" would be. This consciousness would cause for The Only "I" to do. The Only "I" would actually be consciousness. When The Only "I" would be there, The Only "I", then, would be of conscious of The Only "I" to do 'Will'. So doing would depend upon 'beingness' of doer. All other verbs are actually other forms of 'Do' which would reveal 'doingness' of various doings. So, where 'being' would be there, there would be 'doing'."

"So, there would be relation between the Being and the Doing?"

"Yes. The Being wouldn't be the Being without the Doing. The Doing couldn't go on even take breath without the Being."

"Then, how would the 'Be', the first basic character, be the male and the 'Do', second basic character, be the Female?"

Chapter-8

"Both the male being and the female being would be one and another one of each and every 'I'. Both are they who have cherished the Illusion in their basic qualities separately. Who has cherished the Illusion in the quality of 'Be' less than in the quality of 'Do' would be the male being."

"What is the main reason for each and every "I" to be as the Male being due to have cherished the Illusion in the quality of 'Be' less than in the quality of 'Do'?"

"Doing of 'Will' of The Only "I" would cause each and every 'I' to be as each and every 'I' and to do something or some other thing again and again to be The Only "I". At the same time among doings of the male being and the female being, the male being would cause the female being to retain its femininity by means of which the body, comprised of the WORLD would be made of, for each and every 'I' who would enter into that body in course of Regaining the Unlost. So, whoever would cause another one to do one's own would ever be the Male i.e that does not give birth to offspring and another one who would be caused to do another one's would ever be the Female i.e. that produces offspring. Because the 'Do' as the main verb does only one thing i.e. doing whereas as the auxiliary verbs it (do) would help all other verbs which are actually forms of the 'Do'. At the same time, the Male being would do all its doings and would cause the Female being to do its doings to retain its femininity."

"Then, for its one more doing than the Female doing, why is the Male being termed as the Male being whereas doings of each and every 'I' are greater in number than that of The Only "I"?"

'Because, the Causing. Like The Only "I" who would cause for doings of each and every 'I', the Male being would cause for doings of the Female being to retain its femininity."

"So, the cause would only be the reason?"

"Yes."

"When the Male being would cause the Female being to retain its femininity, isn't the causing of the Male being a doing?"

"Yes. Both the Causing and the Effecting of the cause are certainly doings. But when the female being would receive the effect by the cause of the male being, its femininity would be got fruitful. When it would be got so, it would have to do more doings than the male being."

"If the Female being would be caused and got fruitful, then, would its Illusion recede or vanish?"

"Being caused would be physically, mentally, spiritually; physically and spiritually; physically and mentally; mentally and spiritually; physically, mentally and spiritually separately and physically, mentally and spiritually collectively."

"Wouldn't being caused be done at a time physically, mentally, spiritually ; physically and mentally; physically and spiritually; mentally and spiritually; physically, mentally and spiritually separately and physically, mentally and spiritually collectively ?"

"No, many a time it wouldn't be. Though both Male and

Female beings make efforts with their best, it couldn't be possible at all times."

"Why?"

"Because, in their course of doings, both would ever be affected by the 'Will'."

"Will? The acronym of Worship, Image, Language and Law?"

"No, It is another 'Will' an acronym of World, Ignorance, Life and Lust."

"When all those beings would have to go on in the World, how would they be affected by the World ?"

"All the beings i.e. the male human beings and the female human beings would cherish that the World is the Truth and in it only they could achieve their end actually what It is none of them could know and learn and they would go on while cherishing the Illusion that the World is only the Truth?"
"Isn't the World the Truth?"

"No, it is the Untruth at the same time it is the Truth."

"How it is?"

"When The Only "I" do 'Will' to be Many, then only, the World comes into existence and lasts for some span of time. After termination of that lasting-span of time of the World, The Only "I" do 'Will' not to be 'Many', then, that World would merge into The Only "I". As long as the World would last as existing it is the Truth and when It would merge into The Only "I" and wouldn't have Its own existence until The Only "I" would do 'Will' again, then during the span of Its non-existence It is the Untruth."

"Would all these beings go on and do their doings ignorantly?"

"Yes. They would."

"How?"

"They would assume that they wouldn't be The Only "I" and they have been created by The Only "I"."

"What is wrong with that assumption?"

"They would assume that they would receive the reward or the retribution for their doings done during their breathing after the last breath of them."

"Wouldn't they receive so and so?"

"They would. But they themselves would confer either the reward or the retribution on themselves only."

"Do they do so and so? But how?"

"Because, each and every 'I' who have been in the bodies of the beings, would not be other than The Only "I". Each and every 'I', who would cherish the Illusion that each and every 'I' would be other than The Only "I", would be so ignorant. So cherishing the Illusion that each and every 'I' would be beyond The Only "I" or other than The Only "I" would only be the 'ignorance'.

"How would the life affect the beings?"

"All the beings would cherish that the life of them wouldn't end, though they would watch ending of life of neighboring being, or life would long as much long period as they wish."

"Upon which or whom the longness of the life of them would depend?"

"Upon their own doings. That doings sometimes would enable the life to long for some extent or some other extent or sometimes might enable the life to long for some long or some other long. But the beings couldn't know and learn that they would have many lives which would begin, long for some long, end and begin and thus they repeat again and again."

"Why would those lives repeat alike ?"

"In consequence of their own rewards or retributions, the beings would receive their repeated lives."

"Would each and every life be one and the same ?"

"Never. As per rewards or retributions the lives of the human beings would be. The lives of a human being, in consequence of its doings, would or might be of a sort of being another sort of being, some other sort of being like so of so many sorts of beings respectively and later can be of human being would be assessed."

"What about the lust ?"

"It is the very strong feeling of sexual desire."

"What is wrong with it?"

"When a male being or a female would be impacted by the lust, it would even assault or decline itself to fulfill its sexual desire with opposite-sex while ignoring relationship, proper time, place, circumstances, age etc. in course of indulging its bodily-senses."

"What would be happened to it, if it does so ?"

"Its ignoring such and such would cause it to receive retributions."

"Wouldn't be there possibility for rewards?"

"As long as it would behave alike in course of indulging bodily senses, it couldn't ever receive rewards."

"What about opposite-sex which would be assaulted ?"

"If the being of opposite-sex stoops to the assault, then, it would also receive retributions only."

"If the being of opposite-sex doesn't stoop but fails to face, then?"

"Then what other else for its willful (at its will) of non-stooping, rewards for its facing would be better life in forthcoming incarnation."

Chapter-9

"Would I receive a reward or a retribution for my looking at You amorously ?"

"You must receive a retribution for Your that doing ."

"In this context what does retribution mean?"
"Not only in this context, each and every context in which a doing, which ought not to be done, is done. The Retribution would be imposed on the doer. The Retribution means a fair punishment which might have been in various forms."

"Wouldn't You take share in the Retribution ?"

"Not at all."

"Why ?"

"Because, I have not got such feeling that is to receive Your looking."

"Would You receive reward for Your not receiving?"

"No, I wouldn't."

"When I receive a Retribution, why wouldn't You receive a reward in vice – versa?"

"Not-receiving Your amorous looking at me is not my doing which I intended to do."

"Isn't Your not-receiving a doing ?"

"Yes. It is indubitably a doing. But it wasn't done with my 'Will'. So, it is not a part of my own 'Will'."

"It may not be a part of Your 'Will', But it was a doing of You. So, You are a doer. For every doing, there would be a meed. Wouldn't be there?"

"Yes. There would be a meed. But it wouldn't be reward but Benediction of The "I"."

"Benediction of The "I"! What is It?"

"Benediction is that The Only "I", Myself, bestow some favour on One when The "I" please."

"Do The "I" please?"

"Yes. "I" do."

"How? The "I" am only the Spectator of all doings done by each and every "I". Amn't The "I"?"

"Yes. The "I" am only the Spectator of all doings of each and every 'I'. Whenever any each and every 'I' don't do anything as a part of 'Will', then only, The "I" do bestow. Whenever any each and every 'I' do anything as a part of own 'Will' it means 'Will' of that each and every 'I', then, that each and every 'I' only either bestow reward or impose retribution upon that each and every 'I'."

"If so, isn't there scope for that each and every 'I' to bestow reward only on that each and every 'I' as that each and every

'I' am only that each and every 'I'?"

"No. Scope isn't there. Because each and every 'I' am not such each and every 'I' who am beyond or apart from each and every 'I'. You must keep in Your mind that in each and every 'I' there would be "I" i.e. The Only "I" of whom 'Will' only The Only "I", Myself, would be each and every 'I' as the bit of The Only "I".

"Amn't each and every 'I' separated from The Only "I" ?"

"Not at all. There would never be the existence for each and every 'I' in separation. Each and every 'I' do cherish like that only."

"Then how could each and every 'I' do 'will' of each and every 'I'?"

"Because, each and every 'I' am not at all any other beyond or apart from The Only "I". When The Only "I" do 'Will', each and every 'I' also do 'will'. But as long as each and every 'I' would go on as each and every 'I' in consequence of cherishing the Illusion, each and every 'I' do 'will' under impact of that Illusion due to which each and every 'I' couldn't be Omnipotent to do any as each and every 'I' do wish. Besides, under that impact each and every 'I' couldn't be Omniscient to decide which is asset to each and every 'I' beyond the Judgement for proper justification."

"So,"

"So only, The "I" would pass Judgement which would ever be proper justification for the doings of those who are in opposite sides or more sides."

"How could the retribution affect upon that each and every 'I' who would receive so?"

"Every each and every 'I' have been doing the Practice to achieve the target i.e. to regain what actually each and every 'I' have not lost. But the most of them might have not expressed what is target and what is being done out. This doing of them would have been affected."

"How could, that target and doing for that to be achieved, be affected?"

"They would ignore absolutely that they ought to regain what they have not lost and they would do again and again the things which keep them under the Illusion what they cherished in the earlier."

Chapter-10

"Then, what will happen?"

"Now, You are looking at me amorously without any supposition. This doing would give You sense-pleasure."

"What is wrong with this sense-pleasure?"

"Sense-pleasure is of the body but not of 'I' i.e. not of You who are an each and every 'I'.

"Again what is wrong?"

"Body is a means to each and every 'I' to do Practice but that body is not at all each and every 'I' though the body is made of five elements which have been emerged from The Only "I" and they are too in fact The Only "I". As long as each and every 'I' would get pleased with sense-pleasure, each and every 'I' would go on as each and every 'I' only."

"Once again what is wrong?"

"This sense- pleasure would affect the Practice of each and every 'I'."

"How would that affecting be?"

"This affecting would lead each and every 'I' not to be gracious enough to receive the human body."

"So what?"

"Except the human being, all other beings are Voluptuous-beings."

"Voluptuous-beings ? What are they?"

"Voluptuous-beings are those which would always tend towards the gratification of the sense or the indulgence of the physical appetites."

"What will be wrong if they are let do so?"

"They could not be as Voluptuous beings up to the end of Creation i.e. doing of 'Will' of The Only "I" not to be 'Many'."

"How long could they be?"

"Though their longness of The Only "I" would decide in course of bestowing or extending kindness, time and time the most of them couldn't preserve their longness."

"Who could ruin their longness?"

"Some of them could do of another some."

"Why do some of them would do alike?"

"Owing to their appetite, they would do so."

"Then, what will happen to them?"

"They couldn't get the bodies required to them as per their own deeds."

"Then, can't they go on as beings?"

"They could go on as beings?"

"Without bodies?"

"Without body, no being could go on as the being."

"Then, how can they get bodies required?"

"They couldn't get required bodies as per their deeds done."

"Then?"

"Then, they would enter into human bodies only."

"Then what is wrong?"

"Body can be of the human but the entity can't be of the human."

"Is it possible?"

"There would be no other way. The entity would be of that being of which sort it would have to be but the body would be of human."

"You mean?"

"The being must be of its own sort but could be in the form of human."

"What will be the wrong with the being of the entity other than human enter into the body of human?"

"As long as the being which would be in the body of human

body could behave like human being in having food, taking sleep, getting fear and participating in the copulating but couldn't exercise or utilize distinctiveness in above doings. As a indweller of human body it can speak which is too in imitating manner only."

"What is imitating manner?"

"In imitating, either self-thought or self-practice couldn't be."

"Let it do imitation. What's wrong?"

"Imitation sounds that absence of self-practice. Each and every human being is ever expected to do Practice itself of its own."

"Despite absence of self-practice too, can't it be the Practice when it acts like another by imitating?"

"No, it could never be the Practice."

"Why?"

"Without 'WILL', doing i.e. imitating couldn't be the Practice."

"What relevance is there to the Practice to 'WILL'?"

"Nothing could be the Practice without Worshipping, Image to be worshipped, Language to be spoken to worship and Law to be abided by."

Chapter-11

"Who worships whom?"

"The Player-'I' worships the Believer-in 'I'."

"If the Player-'I' don't worship the Believer-in 'I', what will happen to the Player-'I' and to the Believer-in 'I' ?"

"When the Player-'I' don't worship the Believer-in 'I', then, the Believer-in 'I' wouldn't do grace the Player-'I'."

"If the Believer-in 'I' don't grace the Player-'I', what will happen to the Player -'I'?"

"Then, the Player-'I' would need to go on as the Player-'I' without getting any proficiency in regaining that which that Player-'I' haven't actually lost."

"Again What will happen to the Player-'I'?"

"That Player-'I' go on as that Player-'I' up to The Only "I" do 'Will' not to be 'Many'."

"Afterwards?"

"When The Only "I" do 'Will' not to be 'Many', all bits of each and every 'I' would remain attached to the Deeds and the Matter which is in Many forms comprising of atoms and in other forms not comprising of any atoms would merge into The Only "I"."

"When all these remained attached to and all those the Matter would merge into The Only "I" in consequence of doing 'Will' not to be Many of The Only "I" and all they and they would get their and their existence lost, why do the bit of each and every 'I' need to do the Practice?"

"In that form (each and every 'I') of The Only "I" in which form there would be The Only "I" too, The Only "I" would have each and every casual body of each and every bit of each and every 'I'."

"Casual body ! What is it? Then, how could The Only "I" be addressed or acknowledged as The Only "I"?"

"Casual body is not a body like a body made of five elements even it is not a body which is made of 'Supposition' which has induced each and every bit of each and every 'I' to be each and every 'I' but not The Only "I"."

"Doesn't this Casual body itself have its own existence separately from The Only "I" when The Only "I" do 'Will' 'not to be Many' and would go on as The Only "I" when there wouldn't be bits of each and every 'I', atoms of forms of Matter and those forms which wouldn't comprise of atoms of Matter?"

"No, the Casual body wouldn't have existence separately. Even this Casual body wouldn't be among those which would be seemed as bits of each and every 'I' and the Matter which would be in two sorts i.e. a sort which would be comprised of atoms and another sort which wouldn't be comprised of atoms."

"While the 'Many' go on, where would this Casual body there?"

"Along with remaining bodies i.e. Micro bodies (subtle-bodies) and Macro bodies (gross bodies)."

"Would Microbodies and Macrobodies only merge?"

"Yes. There You are."

"But. You have just told that this Casual body wouldn't be among bits of each and every 'I' and the Matter of both sorts. How that?"

"The Casual body would be neither a bit of each and every 'I' nor any sort of Matter to which both The Only "I" would be beyond during the Many goes on."

"Then, would the Casual body be with The Only "I"?"

"The Casual body would be only The Only "I"."

"When The Only "I" would be beyond each and every bit of each and every 'I' and The Only "I" would only be the Casual body, how could the Casual body be along with Micro bodies and Macro bodies of all bits of each and every 'I'?"

"The Only "I" would be Omnipotent. So only The Only "I" could be as The Only "I" beyond all bits of each and every 'I' and all sorts of the 'Many' i.e. sorts of those which would be comprised of atoms and of those which wouldn't and could be the Casual bodies of each and every bit of each and every 'I'."

"What would this Casual body do during the 'Will' either to be 'Many' or 'not to be Many' done by The Only "I"?"

"As the Casual body, The Only "I" would be the Spectator for each and every doing being done by each and every 'I' and would be of each and every aftermath of that doing and the consequences of each and every aftermath too."

"What would The Only "I" do with that of aftermath and consequence of that aftermath?"

"When The Only "I" do 'Will' to be 'Many' on termination of duration of the 'Will' 'not to be 'Many' done, those bits of each and every 'I' who could be 'accountable' for aftermaths and consequences of their doings would be graced to resume their Practice to regain what they haven't actually lost."

Chapter-12

"Who would do grace?"

"None otherelse. Whoever is accountable."

"Would each and every bit of each and every I' do grace each and every bit of each and every 'I'?"

"Yes."

"How? That, whoever is accountable, be so thatself ?"

"Yes. The Casual body of each and every 'I' Myself recline until and unless The Only "I" again do 'Will' to be 'Many'. When The Only "I" do 'Will' to be 'Many', then, the Casual body of each and every 'I' would grace each and every 'I' according to the doings of each and every 'I' done during the 'Will' of The Only "I" to be 'Many' had been carried through previously."

"Would the gracing of each and every of Casual body be analogous or resemblant or connate or sundry or miscellaneous with that of any other Casual body?"

"Never. To achieve Oneness is the end of each and every 'I'."

"With whom?"

"With any another one of each and every 'I'."

"How could it be possible?"

"Observing the Practice."

"When there wouldn't be the same gracefulness bestowed upon at least two bits of each and every 'I', could a bit of each and every 'I' achieve Oneness with any other bit of each and every 'I' upon whom the gracefulness would be very proximity to?"

"Even with that which would be long-drawn-out too."

"Could that?"

"Positively, indubitably and evidently."

"Could the Casual body really do grace?"

"Once again You are boggling. The Casual body could do it."

"Why don't 'I' do so instead of the Casual body?"

"Already it has been told that the Casual body of each and every 'I' would be only The Only "I". Both The Only "I" and the Casual body of each and every 'I' would ever be one and the same."

"Yes. It has been already told. But why don't I get reckoned that both the_Casual body and The Only "I" would be one and the same?"

"Your cherishing the Illusion, that You and The Only "I" would be separated from each and other, would be affecting to get reckoned so."

Chapter-13

"But I have decided to look at You amorously."

"That is Your problem, but I don't receive Your such look."

"Then, what shall I do?"

"You can quest for such one of each and every 'I' who can receive Yours."

"I don't quest for some other though I could."

"Why don't You do?"

"Because, at very first nanosecond when 'I' have seen You, instinctively I have cast such amorous look."

"So only I don't receive such look. Without supposition anything must not be happened."

"Why don't You suppose to receive mine?"

"Very next nanosecond or after such a long, I may receive such look cast on me by any other one of each and every 'I' but not Yours."

"Why don't receive mine only?"

"In previous duration of 'Will' done by The Only "I", there might have some association which had been adhered to my Casual body."

"Then what about the association which had been adhered to my Casual body ?"

"To receive anything, the adhered association to the Casual body must be there."

"To demand, request, ask etc. mustn't it be requisite?"

"To demand, request, ask etc. is Your doing at present and the then too."

"Isn't there any relation with the Casual body regarding demanding, asking etc.?"

"The Casual body is adhered to what You do and how You do and Your intention of Your doing. The resulted in of Your doing, way of doing and intention of doing would be adhered to Casual body and this Casual body would grace You accordingly."

"Isn't my looking at You amorously a part of 'gracing'?

"The Casual body has graced You to see, look, watch etc. But casting amorous look is Your doing done without supposition."

"Wouldn't amorous looking too be a part of gracing of the Casual body?"

"Never. It wouldn't be."

"Why?"

"Looking is a doing whereas amorous looking is a doing

done with intention."

"Shouldn't Looking with intention be done?"

"Should be done when Your counterpart would also intent like same how and what You do."

Chapter-14

"What would happen if You receive though You don't intent?"

"When I succumb to You without my own intention, I will be held amenable for giving scope to You to commit undesirable doing and defile my own Practice and let both of us affect Practice of those who have relation with both of us."

"To the extent of both of us it might be accepted but regarding those who have relation with us, how can it be done?"

"If they are disclosed my succumbing to Your amorous looking cast on me, lot of scope would be there that they would at least, view it on their minds or talk about it."

"Let them do whatever they would."

"Recollect ! what You have just told i.e. 'Let them do whatever they do."

"Yes. I have done. So what?"

"Both doings of us i.e. Your amorous looking cast on me and my succumbing to it would pave the way to them to do some doings i.e. viewing and talking without their initiation and they would hold answerable for those done without their own intention."

"When there is no intention, how would they be held answerable?"

"Each and every doing contains the Mind, the Speech and the Deed. In these their doings their Mind and Speech would be there. So, they would have to hold answerable."

"Can anyone of each and every 'I' maintain not to do any though such one would be let do like them?"

"Yes. Someone or Someone else can do so. Like that Someone or Someone else I am at present making efforts. In such course of Practice only I don't like to receive Yours."

Chapter-15

"Oh! What a looking of You at me?"

"Are You pleased with my looking at You?"

"No. I am not."

"But. You have expressed Your 'Surprise' which may denote Your pleasing."

"Yes. I have expressed my Surprise. But it is not of pleasing but alluring."

"Alluring !"

"Yes."

"In Your alluring, isn't there Your pleasing ?"

"No, there isn't."

"How can You say that You haven't been pleasing?"

"Because, Your amorous looking at me has stirred my sensual body only, but not my mind."

"Does Your alluring receive my looking at You?"

"No, it doesn't."

"But You have told that You were allured due to my looking at You."

"Yes. I have been allured but not due to Your looking but Your amorousness."

"Is looking varied with Amorousness."

"Absolutely."

"How that?"

"Looking could be free from all adjectives which qualify it."

"When 'Looking at' one would be free from all adjectives, Why would 'Looking at' be done?"

"To know and learn."

"If amorousness precedes 'Looking at', what will happen?"

"When You cast Your looking on me with amorousness, it will divulge that You are thirsty for lust."

"What is wrong with me when I feel lust after You?"

"But I do never feel lust after You."

"Do You feel so after any other one of each and every 'I'?"

"No, I do never so after any other one of each and every 'I'."

"Why don't You do so after so?"

"Without Love I don't invite any?"

"Whom do You Love?"

"Who could cast Love on me by dint of any means, then, I may think it over."

"Why won't You make sure You would invite that one of each and every 'I' who cast Love on You?"

"Before inviting that Love, I will have to comprehend genuineness of Love and sincerity of that one."

"Actually what is Love?"

"Love would ever be for sake of Love only."

"Could You explicate it ?"

"Yes. Listen to me.

Whoever its haver may be,
Love ever loves Love only.

Haver might be beautiful,
It could never be enticed.

Might be more affluence,
It could never be surrendered.

Could have absolute authority,
It could never be the slave.

Let it be inbred exhaustive educated,
It could never slavishly rely on.

Haver would ever be a haver of all
But for Love only a supporter at all."

"Yes. I agree with You that Love ought to Love the Love only. But what will be wrong with You if You invite my amorousness which divulges my thirsty for lust to fulfill my sexual desire without casting Your Love on me?"

"Why ought I to fulfill Your sexual desire?"

"Because, You can do that. Can't You ?"

"Not only I can but each and every 'I' also can do so."

"Then, what is objection to You to do mine ?"

"It is not an objection but it is my obligation."

"To whom the obligation You would be under ?"

"To some other each and every 'I' the obligation I would be under. But that one of each and every 'I' have not yet approached."

"Until then, don't You receive mine?"

"No, I don't."

Chapter-16

"Oh ! Your looking at me is so amorous Isn't it ?"

"What do You mean ?"

"I mean I have been fascinated by Your amorous looking."

"Have You been done by either my looking or my amorousness or me only."

"Only by Your amorousness."

"Why have You been done by my amorousness ?"

"I view lookings of all along with Yours as one and the same."

"Can't You find any distinction between any two lookings ?"

"I may or can. But I don't."

"Why don't You do ?"

"I can view each and every looking in such manner which could find what feeling that looking casts on me or any other."

"Then, why don't You take that feeling into consideration ?"

"I don't need any other feeling than amorousness."

"If You find any other feeling than amorousness in any looking ?"

"Immediately, I avert my eyes from that looking."

"Do You notice whose looking is it ?"

"Many a time, I don't."

"When do You notice such one ?"

"When I encounter any incongruous nuance in amorous looking, I shall do then."

"Can each and every amorous looking be same all in all ?"

"Yes. Amorousness would always be amorousness."

"Is it never absorbed into another or another into it?"

"No, it can be mixed with any other but not be absorbed into."

"What is difference between absorbing and mixing?"

"When the amorousness is absorbed into any other, it will get lost its Macro-form whereas it mixes with any other its Macro-form could be preserved as it is."

"So, there would be scope for amorousness to mix with another and be mixed with another."

"Yes."

"Which do You prefer to?"

"You mean?"

"I mean amorousness mixed with or be mixed with any other ?"

"At all events I prefer to amorousness which is free from all others."

"If there is any other mixed with, then, what will happen?"

"I never let my mind pour my own feelings and share them with others."

"Why don't You let ?"

"Many a time I couldn't be sure whether any one of feelings could be equal in same one of my counterpart's feelings."

"If any one of Yours be equal in, what will happen?"

"Scope can be there for an association to be adhered to my own Casual body or to my counterpart's or to both of us."

"Wouldn't there be any scope for the association to be done to Your or Your counterpart's or to both of us, when only amorousness of You and Your meet ?"

"Scope must be there. That association must be pertaining to the Deed only but not to the Mind or the Speech or both the Mind and the Speech."

"Why do You wish such association only which pertaining to the deed ?"

"When The Only "I" do 'Will' to be 'Many' after termination of 'not to be 'Many', then, the Casual body will bestow upon me accordingly."

"How would the bestowing upon You be ?"

"I would have to attend more and more Deeds during the Period."

"What about the Mind and the Speech ?"

"Scope for them to be exercised may not be or may be but little."

Chapter-17

"Have You got any feeling when You received my amorous looking ?"

"No. I haven't."

"But, You received my amorous looking. Didn't You ?"

"Yes. I did."

"Then, how could You haven't got ?"

"I have been allured."

"When You being allured, can't You get feeling ?"

"Never."

"How ?"

"My sensual body or organs have only been allured by Your such looking."

"Wouldn't those be enough to be allured for You to feel whenever You receive amorous looking ?"

"No, those wouldn't make me feel ?"

"Which would make You so ?"

"Whenever my intellect or spirit be either allured or affected then only I do feel."

"If intellect or spirit doesn't get allured but only sensual get done, then, what will happen ?"

"As long as the intellect doesn't get allured, I could go on as the Homo sapien."

"How does the Homo sapien behave ?"

"The Homo sapien behaves while applying mind whereas all other beings do without applying their minds."

"Don't all other beings have their own minds ?"

"They might have their own minds but they haven't intellect to apply the mind."

"Is intellect necessary to apply the mind ?"

"Yes."

"Then, for why do they have their own minds ?"

"To feel something or something else."

"What do they feel ?"

"They feel pleasure, hungry, lust, affection towards their own progeny etc."

"Don't they need intellect to be applied to feel what You tell ?"

"No, their minds themselves do feel."

"Then, why don't Homo sapiens do like ?"

"Homo sapiens too can do like them."

"Then, why do Homo sapiens apply their minds to do so ?"

"Homo sapiens are not only Homo sapiens but Ritualistic-beings also."

"Why are Homo sapiens called as Ritualistic-beings ?"

"Homo sapiens are ever expected to do each and thing purposefully."

"Why are they done alike ?"

"Because, Homo sapiens are bestowed upon with intellect which distinguishes Homo sapiens from Voluptuous beings."

"Can't Homo sapiens behave like Voluptuous beings ?"

"All Homo sapiens beings could behave like Voluptuous beings and Ritualistic beings."

"When do they behave as Homo sapien beings ?"

"Whenever they can do as I am now behaving with You, as Homo sapien beings they must apply mind for their intellect not to be affected."

"When You don't let Your mind not to be affected, what would You achieve ?"

"Then, I must keep not to be guilty of incestuous."

Chapter-18

"Is it necessary to consider incest ?"

"Yes. It is necessary."

"Why ?"

"Then, that Homo sapien being behaves like Voluptuous being which can be affected by hunger, sleep, fear and copulation only. But it couldn't be capable to behave like itself i.e. Homo sapien being which is bestowed upon to exercise its distinctiveness."

"What is the distinctiveness ?"

"By dint of distinctiveness the Homo sapien being observes the relation lies between that to which it behaves and itself."

"Does relation lies between or among Homo sapiens?"

"Yes. It does."

"Is it mandatory to observe relation with any or some or all ?"

"Yes. It is mandatory."

"Is the relation reality to be observed or the respect to be honoured?"

"The relation is truly real. So, it must be observed and honoured accordingly."

"How can You have understood that the relation is truly real ?"

"For each and every doing of each and every 'I', there must be something to be resulted in. This resulted something or something else in must effect or affect one, some, many or each and every doing of one, some, many of each and every 'I'. That or those which would affect must pay the price to that or those which would be affected. That or those which would effect must be paid the price by that or those that which be effected. In course of paying price, the relation in the form of kinship or relationship would be made between or among those who effect or affect and who would be effected or affected accordingly."

"Who decides the kinship or relationship between or among ?"

"Whoeverelse? The casual body of each and every 'I'?"

"For what purpose?"

"First of all to check and control sexual intercourse."

"When there would be only two-chief roles to be played by each and every 'I', what would be wrong if sexual intercourse is taken place or occurred between any two of each and every 'I' who am a Player-'I' and who am a Believer-in 'I' ?"

"All relations would be made according to the Practice that is to pay and is to be paid. When the Relation isn't observed, the Price could be multiplied into minimum hundred times to times of crores."

"Then what will happen?"

"Those, who have to pay the Price, would be kept to go on as each and every 'I' during the several or innumerable periods of 'to be Many' of the 'Will' done by The Only 'I' each one of which follow each one period of 'Not to be Many' of the 'Will' done by The Only 'I'."

"Can't each of each and every 'I' be pleased in any period while breathing with Macro and Micro bodies ?"

"Can't. No each and every 'I' be done."

"Why?"

"Except the form of the Bliss, no any other feeling could last for any long in which each and every 'I' either pleased or worried."

Chapter-19

"When the relation or kinship is observed in the form of Homo sapien being, can any one of each and every 'I' get the form of the Bliss?"

"Unless and until any one of each and every 'I' become Ritualistic being and behave alike that each and every 'I' even can't imagine what is the form of the Bliss."

"If any one of each and every 'I' behave as a Homo sapien being only, then,?"

"As long as any one of each and every 'I' behave as Homo sapien being that each and every 'I' can get enjoyed the behaving of another one of each and every 'I' who also behave as Homo sapien being."

"Do another one of each and every 'I' too get enjoyed like one of each and every 'I' do?"

"Yes. No doubt about it."

"Then, what is the Problem?"

"For one of each and every 'I' am to find out another one of each and every 'I' who behave on equality with one of each and every 'I' and for another one of each and every 'I' am to do alike, would be the problem."

"Could observing either relationship or kinship be helpful for one of each and every 'I' to find out another one of each and every 'I' who behave on equality with one of each and every 'I'?"

"Certainly. But that helpful might be directly or indirectly."

"How would that be?"

"Helpful directly means observing 'Kinship' between one of each and every 'I' and another one of each and every 'I' and behaving accordingly. Helpful indirectly means observing 'relationship' between one of each and every 'I' and another one of each and every 'I' and behaving accordingly."

"What is difference between kinship and relationship ?"

"Kinship means relationship by the blood i.e. relationship established being born from same uterus (womb). Those, who are born from same uterus (womb), are uterine brothers and sisters. For these uterine brothers or sisters to be born those, who would cause, are parents . The relationship among these uterine sisters, brothers and their parents is 'kinship'. This kinship would be also directly or indirectly too."

"How?"

"To observe kinship with uterine brothers and sisters of Parents and children of them is the direct kinship."

"What about relationship other than kinship?"

"Whenever a Player-'I' marry to a Believer-in 'I', that is too the relationship which causes for kinship. The relationship which is established by wedding is termed as wed-lock."

"How should this wedded-couple observe the relationship ?"

"Both are ever permitted to observe any kind of relationship. They can behave like friends, preacher and disciple, master and servant while behaving as wife and husband but not simultaneously."

"Not simultaneously ! How would that be ?"

"While husband and wife behave as Preacher and Disciple or Master and Servant etc., both can be let behave accordingly. After such behaving having got completed, then, both could be let behave as husband and wife on terms prescribed."

"Terms?"

"Yes. No husband and wife are ever permitted to copulate or make love etc. before others. Even They must not give at any cost for any others to watch their copulating or making love directly or indirectly by any means. Because then only there would be least possibility for them not to be affected. Even that love making couldn't be the love making by dint of which that husband and wife couldn't achieve such progress which leads to regain the unlost besides both must be accustomed to fall into beastliness which is the state of Voluptuous beings."

"Is there any other relation other than above?"

"When any two of each and every 'I' behave with each other for any reason, then, it would be a relationship between them. Alike when more than two of each and every 'I' behave with one another for any reason, then, it would also be a relationship among them."

"For why these relationships are established ?"

"Either to strengthen or fortify both items of the Practice of each and every Player-'I' and each and every Believer-in 'I'."

Chapter-20

"What is the indirect kinship ?"

"Whenever any two of each and every 'I' or more than two of each and every 'I' whether they may be only Players -'I' or Believers in 'I' or Player 'I' and Believer-in 'I' or Player-'I' and Players-'I' or Believer-in 'I' and Believer –in 'I' are brought into contact with any reason and behave like those who have uterine relationship and treat each other or one another as uterine relatives, that relationship between or among them is indirect kinship."

"You mean they aren't uterine relatives. Don't You ?"

"Yes. I do mean so."

"The indirect kinship is acknowledging only. Isn't it ?"

"Yes. You are correct. That is acknowledging."

"Then, do You let Your mind to be affected by those relatives who are being acknowledged as uterine relatives ?"

"I do never."

"Why ?"

"Because, they are being treated uterine."

"They may be done. But they aren't genuine. Are they ?"

"Though they aren't genuine uterine relatives, they must

be treated, regarded, honoured and observed like genuine uterine relatives. Henceforth they are uterine relatives for each other or one another."

"Why should, those, who aren't in true uterine relatives but being treated alike, be done like genuine uterine relatives ?"

"Because, treating, regarding, honouring and observing would be done by the Mind and the Speech of doers."

"If not, what will happen ?"

"The Casual body would be adhered to that affecting."

"Then, what will happen ?"

"Doer, then, would have to pay more Price for that. So, doer would go on as doer until the Price is paid."

"In which way the doer ought to pay that Price ?"

"The Casual body of each and every doer would ever be mindful of all doings, tell off misdoings, quantify those and those doings and reckon as well as judge them accurately. Basing on its judgement, in the form of the Casual body only that doer i.e. each and every 'I' could procreate each and every 'I' only but not same each and every 'I' who was as same as in previous incarnation. This procreated each and every 'I' can be either Voluptuous being or Homo sapien being or Ritualistic being that puts on Macro body of Homo sapien being."

"I have asked the way for paying the Price. Haven't I ?"

"Yes. You have. I have been also answering to You. Please listen to what I do answer. Not only that doer i.e. each and every 'I' would have to procreate the same doer i.e. same each and every 'I' in form of certain or certain being but also the affected doer i.e. each and every 'I' who was affected would have to procreate the same each and every 'I' i.e. the affected doer in form of certain or certain being in view of doings and doings that the same affected doer had been mindful told off, quantified, reckoned and judged accurately. In such course earlier each and every 'I' would come into contact with later each and every 'I'. In the same way or another way some other each and every 'I' would come into contact with earlier each and every 'I' or later each and every 'I' or some other each and every 'I' would come into contact with earlier or later. Besides, any above each and every 'I' i.e. earlier or later or some other each and every 'I' would come into contact with another each and every 'I' while having above contacts. Thus various relationships in various forms with various doers would be established. To regard, respect, value, behold, honour, venerate, esteem and rever all sorts of relationships accordingly while behaving, acting, deporting, operating, performing and working accordingly with those with whom such relationships would be established is the way to pay the Price i.e. striking out the associations."

Chapter-21

"When You know and learn relationship, kinship and incestuousness, then, how have You been fascinated by my amorousness ?"

"Because, the Casual body of 'I' have been adhered to so many associations resulted in due to doings which 'I' did during so many 'Wills' done by The Only 'I' in course of gracing each and every 'I' to continue the Practice to Regain the Unlost. Those associations have been still chasing this 'I' to behave like Voluptuous being in lieu of Homo sapien being in whose Macro body I have been now. So, I can feel only with the Mind without exercising intellect though I seem even look like Homo sapien being. Owing to such associations, now 'I' am the most vulnerable being to be affected at once and 'I' am very much feeble-minded that couldn't check and control the absorptive extravagant gesticulated dancing of carnal desires which wouldn't be in tunes with any or follow any metre or any metre composed by any."

"Then, what will happen?"

"As a fascinated Homo sapien being which is very feeble-minded, I wouldn't make love to You but I copulate with You lecherously."

"What is difference between making love to me and copulating with me lecherously ?"

"In such copulation, 'I' shall smite You."

"I invite it."

"I know You do it."

"Then, why do You repudiate my offer ?"

"For Homo sapien beings, copulation is never advised or suggested or prescribed."

"Why ?"

"Because, in copulation done, male Voluptuous being seems as if it attacked female being while burning with enimity. It may not seem in each and every Voluptuous being."

"Does female being invite it ?"

"There is no question of inviting but being suppressed to the lust of itself or of male being."

"Is 'Suppression' accepted by female being ?"

"The term 'Suppression' itself sounds the victim-participator i.e. female being would 'spurn' at all."

"What would be wrong with male being when it suppresses female being and female being when it spurns male being ?"

"As far as concerned with the Voluptuous beings, no wrong would be with them whenever male suppresses female and female spurns male. In fact a male Voluptuous being doesn't suppress a female and a female doesn't spurn a male."

Chapter-22

"Then?"

"As far as concerned with Homo sapien being in which an each and every 'I' whose entity would be of Voluptuous being, then, the Problem would be there."

"What would be the Problem?"

"It couldn't be defined beyond question."

"Why ?"

"Because, a male Homo sapien being can be with entity of a sort of Voluptuous being and a female Homo sapien being can be with entity of another sort of Voluptuous being. If the copulation is done between these male Homo sapien being and female Homo sapien being, then, there would be Suppression and Spurning instead of reciprocal elegant enjoying that must be equal in all levels and ranges."

"Though a male Homo sapien being may be with entity of a sort of Voluptuous being and a female Homo sapien being may be with entity of another sort of Voluptuous being, they have Macro bodies of Homo sapien beings only. Then, how couldn't they achieve such achievement when they have same organs of sex that Homo sapien beings do have?"

"By means of exerting such organs of sex only, no male and no female would take delight in copulation by no means or by some means or other. Even both organs couldn't get their heat of passion slaked. Moreover their heat of passion would get increased at once when they finish copulation again which would increase that heat. Thus that heat would never get quenched."

"When that heat of passion isn't quenched, what will happen?"

"Along with existing associations, other associations would be adhered to the Casual bodies of male Homo sapien being and female Homo Sapien being."

"When that male Homo sapien being and that female Homo sapien being do have entities of a sort and of another sort of Voluptuous beings, how their Casual bodies would be adhered to associations?"

"Because, those male Homo sapien being and female Homo sapien being are indwellers in Macro bodies of Homo sapien being though their entities aren't of Homo sapien being."

Chapter-23

"Why couldn't it be possible to that male and that female who are the indwellers in Homo sapien to quench that heat of passion by exerting organs of sex of Homo sapien which they do have ?"

"Homo sapien beings are commanded to delight in the love making, which must lead Homo sapien beings to have intercourse, which means not only sexual connexion between a man and a woman but the dealings between individuals and exchanges of ideas also. Employing organs of sex is a pretext to male and female beings of Homo sapien. Therefore, as indwellers in bodies of Homo sapien beings, those Voluptuous beings could never perform love making. They would copulate with each other. So, as indwellers in bodies of Homo sapien, those Voluptuous beings, which are, despite, of same sort too, couldn't quench the heat of passion aroused whenever they would copulate with each other."

"Couldn't those male Voluptuous being and female Voluptuous being which are indwellers in the bodies of Homo sapien, behave like male Homo sapien being and female Homo sapien being which are indwellers in the bodies of Homo sapien only ?"

"Never. They couldn't. Their behaviour itself would imply that they wouldn't be Homo sapien beings though they would appear as beings of Homo sapien due to be indwellers in the bodies of Homo sapien."

"Couldn't those, male Voluptuous being and female Voluptuous being which are indwellers in the bodies of

Homo sapien, act like male Homo sapien being and female Homo sapien being which would indwell in the bodies of Homo sapien only?"

"Some extent they can but they could not. They would act to quench whichever desire it may be. To quench desire is only their purpose. They would never do 'Will' which they even couldn't understand apprehend, grasp, comprehend and conceive even imagine, fancy, guess, suppose and envisage."

"Couldn't those male Voluptuous being and female Voluptuous being which are indwellers in the bodies of Homo sapien, do like male Homo sapien being and female Homo sapien being which are indwellers in the bodies of Homo sapien only ?"

"It might almost be supposed as they do. All beings they may be Ritualistic beings, Homo sapien beings or Voluptuous beings are doers. No doubt about it. Doing means carrying out an 'Action'. Here the point is 'Action'. Action would be of the 'Will' done by 'Self', of the 'Will' done by 'Another Self', of the instruction issued by another or others or of the Pleasure of Self or another or others. It is always kept in mind that 'no being no doing or no doing no being'. After doing 'Will' 'not to be Many' done by The Only "I", then only, it might be seemed there wouldn't be Doing but that Undoing would be too Doing of The Only "I"."

"Then, of which Voluptuous do ?"

"Of the instruction."

"How ? Whoever do instruct them ?"

"Its own associations of a Voluptuous being in its previous incarnations adhered to its Casual body do instruct it to do carry out something or some other things in course of quenching sensual and carnal desires."

"In which way do the associations of it instruct it ?"

"As the associations adhered to the Casual body of it, the Casual body which is too, like Micro and Macro bodies, made of thirty six entities would let its instruction be as 'instinctiveness' that enables the Voluptuous body to do from time to time as a receiver of instruction."

"Are all thirty six entities of Macro, Micro and Casual bodies one and the same?"

"Regarding to the Entity, such one entity of Macro body of a being and same such one entity of Micro and Casual bodies of same being are one and the same, alike remaining entities too but the forms of such one entity of Macro, same such one entity of Micro and same such entity of a body of being would differ from one another. Among them, the form of any such entity of Casual body couldn't be conceived, comprehended, grasped, apprehended and understood to the Homo sapien being even to the Ritualistic being."

"To whom it could be done?"

"To those who would have almost envisioned that they haven't lost to regain."

Chapter-24

"Regarding Micro body?"

"Though Micro body would be made of thirty six entities, it would be in the form of conscienceness which contains four inward senses i.e. the Mind, the Intellect, the Ego and the Pleasure."

"Are the organs of sense and the inward senses one and the same?"

"No, they aren't."

"What are the organs of senses?"

"The organs of senses are five. They are senses of 'Touch', 'Sight', 'Hear', 'Taste' and 'Smell'."

"What is the difference between organs of senses and the inward senses?"

"The organs of senses are barely organs which attract corresponding senses. But required intellect of senses would not be applied to that attracting. So, these senses can be termed as bodily senses of Macro bodies of beings. Regarding inward senses, it must be comprehended that they are of inner nature of Homo sapien beings and Ritualistic beings. So, these senses would be of Micro bodies of Homo sapien beings and Ritualistic beings?"

"Don't Voluptuous beings have these inward senses?"

"They too have these inward senses."

"Then, why haven't You mentioned them along with Homo sapien beings and Ritualistic beings ?"

"Because, the Mind of Voluptuous beings would not have been graced with 'Intellect'."

"Who wouldn't have graced them with 'Intellect'?

"Whoever else? The Casual body of each and every 'I' who have entered into the body made of thirty six entities."

"If so, what would happen to those who have entered into such sort of bodies?"

"They couldn't make up their own Mind as their Mind wouldn't contain 'Intellect'. So they could feel only and respond either involuntary or reflectively in return."

"Regarding Homo sapien beings?"

"Homo sapien beings could make up their own Mind as their Mind would contain 'Intellect'. So, they could feel like Voluptuous beings and respond with 'Intellect'. Their distinction is that when they apply their Mind they could exercise their 'Intellect' and when they exercise their 'Intellect' they would apply their Mind. Even they could exercise their 'Intellect' without applying their Mind."

"Couldn't they apply their Mind without exercising their 'Intellect'?"

"They could do so."

"Don't they do so?"

"Now, You have come on my way. Whenever those Homo sapien beings do so i.e. applying their Mind without exercising their 'Intellect', then, they couldn't be Homo sapien beings but Voluptuous beings though indwell in the bodies of Homo sapien."

"You mean the 'Intellect' only distinguishes Homo sapien beings from Voluptuous beings. Don't You?"

"Yes. I do."

"In the earlier You have told that Macro form of the Atman (the Soul) is the Mind and Micro form of the Mind is the Atman (the Soul)." Haven't You ?"

"Yes. I have."

"Is that Mind, which is Macro form of the Atman (the Soul), same which is the first among inward senses?"

"Yes. That is."

"When the Mind is Macro form of the Atman (the Soul) which is literally The Only "I", how couldn't the Mind of the Voluptuous beings be 'Intellect' when The Only "I" am the Omniscient?"

"The Casual body of the Voluptuous being would adjudge the Voluptuous being to be so."

Chapter-25

"What does the Mind do or how is It used ?"

"As an inward sense, the Mind does determine and fancy."

"What does the Mind determine?"

"Each and every doing would be done by the determination of the Mind."

"Has, You being fascinated by amorousness also, been done by the determination of Your Mind?"

"There You are."

"For Your doing, i.e. being fascinated by my amorousness, why would Your Casual body be adhered to association of such doing when You aren't an actual doer but Your Mind ?"

"My Mind is a Macro-form of the Atman (the Soul), which is the inseparable from The Only "I", the indivisible part of The Only "I" and the 'Intellect', which is literally the science of the Omniscienceness of The Only "I", has been bestowed upon the Mind i.e. my Mind like all Homo sapien beings. So, determination and fancy either simultaneously or separately or one after one of My Mind is the determination and fancy of me only. So only, my Casual body would be adhered to association of such doing when Myself am only an actual doer in lieu of my Mind."

"Would the thing, which has been determined by the Mind, be abiding or provisional ?"

"It can be abiding or provisional."

"If it would be abiding .....?"

"That is the Problem...."

"If it would be provisional .....?"

"That is also the Problem."

"Then, how ?"

"So only, the 'Intellect' has been bestowed upon the Mind."

"How would it be the Problem when the determined thing of the Mind be abiding ?"

"The Mind would determine anything which could affect the Practice. As fascinated by Your amorousness, I could let my Mind determine to copulate with You whenever I wish. Accordingly the Intellect would endorse that determination and decide what the Mind intends. Many a time You can cooperate with me. But every time You can not. Can You ?"

"Yes. I agree with You that every time I may not. At least once I can not or may not. So what ?"

"As the determination and fancy, my Mind doesn't let the Intellect either rescind or review its decision."

"What is that decision ?"

"To indulge in copulation with You while ignoring whether You too can indulge in it or not."

"Why can't I indulge in that ?"

"As a fascinated, my Mind never let my 'Intellect' have

forbearance whenever You don't cooperate with me to copulate with You. I never consider Your request, prayer, entreaty or submission for the copulation to be taken place after very little duration of time also. I never take Your mood, stamina even unsound constitution of Your body into account. Thus I would have to behave with You regarding processing of copulating with You."

"If I don't cooperate with You, what do You do ?"

"I shall make all my efforts overpower You."

"Can You succeed ?"

"I am sure. I can do."

"How are You so? And how can You do so ?"

"Now I am physically stronger than You. So, I am sure. You can not protect Yourself upon my assault by some means or other. So I can do. Do You believe that You are stronger than me so that You can protect Yourself upon my assault ?"

"No, I don't believe. After that what do You do ?"

"I hope that I shall repress all Your emotions."
"How can You hope so ?"

"When I overpower You, I shall provoke You to get Your carnal desires aroused. I can tune You to play cymbal according to my notes. Don't You suppose that I could do so ?"

"I do suppose. Later on what do You do ?"

"When I provoke You, I shall, then, suppress You so that You couldn't protest any activity I do."

"What sort of activities, You would do ?"

"When You are suppressed, since then, instinctively I shall start to treat You as a palatable easement thing to be enjoyed."

"How do You enjoy me ?"

"As wildly as I could."

" 'Wildly' means ?

"Vey abnormally. In such course I treat Your entire body as a delicious dish. I shall nip any part of Your body as per my wish; bite You alike; knead You as above; beat You like wise; lash You identically even flog You equally but can be cruelly."

"By doing so what do You gain ?"

"Nothing I shall gain. Besides I shall get fainted or languished thoroughly."

"When You get languished thoroughly, what will happen to me ?"

"You will too be languished thoroughly, in addition, You can be smitten utterly."

"If so happened to both of us, then.....?"

"Then, both You and I would be remained as inanimate beings though both of us breathe, are sensible, have lives and aren't dead at all."

"Are there inanimate beings ?"

"No, there are inanimate things in lieu of inanimate beings. Inanimate things such as rock etc. are those which wouldn't do the Practice. When You are smitten utterly and I am languished thoroughly, then, both of us couldn't do anything to which both of us would be ennobled to regain what both of us have unlost. Though both of us are, in fact, doers would be Doers of Undoing and Undoers of Doing."

"What is Doing and what is Undoing as You have told that Undoing of The Only "I" is also the Doing ?"

"The best question You have now put. Listen to me. The Only "I" do 'Will' to be 'Many'. Doing 'Will' of The Only "I" to be 'Many' isn't for The Only "I" but for each and every 'I' whose Casual body was there during 'Not to be Many' which The Only "I" did 'Will' and each and every 'I' who cherish Illusion that each and every 'I' am not The Only "I" and away from The Only "I". For both this each and every 'I' and that each and every 'I' to do the Practice, The Only "I" do 'Will'. So, those, who do the Practice meant to regain the Unlost are the doers. Those, who are meant to do the Practice and who ought to do the Practice are only the Undoers who are in such deplorable situation which occurs from their self deeds and in which they couldn't do the Practice meant to regain the Unlost."

"Do these Undoers, who are in said situation, do other things than the Practice ?"

"Yes, they do."

"Then, why don't You receive them as doers ?"

"Because, by doing any other thing than doing the Practice, they don't achieve their Ultimate End at which all kinds of their doings must be completed absolutely. Any doing which is meant to do the Practice only be completed absolutely at the Ultimate End i.e. Regaining the Unlost. Hence, doing the thing other than doing the Practice is 'Undoing' and undoing any thing affects doing the Practice is 'Doing'."

"By Your assault made on me, I might have been smitten utterly. Therefore I couldn't do the Doing meant to the Practice. Then, how could 'I' be adjudged as an undoer of doing and a doer of undoing."

"Your 'amorousness' cast on me when You looked at me, provoked me make assault on You. So You ought to pay such price."

"Can You be exempted from paying price for Your assaulting ?"

"No, I can't be. I ought too to pay price as I would be accountable for You to be a doer of undoing."
"So, both of us ought to do pay. Oughtn't we to ?"

"Yes. Both of us."

Chapter-26

"Hasn't amorousness ever been accepted ?"

"When an each of each and every 'I' who am an indweller in the body of Homo sapien would cast amorous looks on another each of each and every 'I' who am too indweller in the another body of Homo sapien, then, it might be accepted."

" 'Might be' not would be ?"

" 'Would be' too."

" 'Might be' ; because when both bodies are of same sort, then, the assault can be replaced by seduction. The copulation, which is done because of seduction, couldn't be love making which is to be welcome by the Practice."

"What is seduction ?"

"Seduction is also a copulation."

"When both a male Homo sapien being and a female Homo sapien being who are indwellers in the bodies of same sort i.e. of Homo sapien do participate in copulation, how could that seduction is treated as copulation which would be done by Voluptuous beings ?"

"Because, seduction is as same as copulation. If copulation is done between a male Voluptuous being and a female Voluptuous being of same sort, it could ever be treated as copulation which would be done only physically as Voluptuous beings couldn't apply intellect to the Mind, which is in Voluptuous beings, would feel or respond only. In seduction too, a male Homo sapien being and a female Homo sapien being would get indulged in lieu of getting enraptured."

"Then, what is difference between copulation and seduction ?"

"In true, both are One and the Same."

"Then why do You use the term 'copulation' to Voluptuous beings and the term 'Seduction' to human beings i.e. Homo sapien beings ?"

"As far as concerned to the 'copulation' taken place between a male and a female Voluptuous beings, there would be no scope for the Mind to be applied whereas as far as concerned to the 'Seduction' taken place between a male and a female Homo sapien beings, there would be absolute scope for the Mind to be applied."

"Must a male Homo sapien being and a female Homo sapien being need to apply their Minds to copulate each other ?"

"Yes. They must do."

"Why don't both or any one of them apply the Mind ?"

"When bodily senses of both or any one of them get overpowered the Mind, then, both or any one of them succumb to those senses."

"What will be wrong with both or any one of both, if so happened ?"

"Both or any one of both will be held accountable as the Practice of both can be disturbed."

"How can one of both, who has been overpowered, be held accountable ?"

"One of both, who has been overpowered, must not be disturbed in the Practice mentally but physically that must. When comparison is done, one, who has been overpowered, would be less accountable and can be free from that fault within short time i.e. lesser incarnation than that One who has overpowered."

"Would that be justification done to one who has been overpowered ?"

"Yes. That would be."

"How ?"

"In that seduction in which if a male Homo sapien being and a female Homo sapien being are there, both would be accountable for it, because, a seduction wouldn't be a physical intercourse."

"What is the physical intercourse ?"

"In a physical intercourse taken place between a male Homo sapien being and a female Sapien being, there could never be overpowering and succumbing but overpowering each other. Even succumbing too would be overpowering."

"If any one of both would not be so strong enough to be overpowered, then, ?"

"If any one of both would really not so strong enough to be overpowered, it would be too seduction only."

Chapter-27

"Wouldn't a female Voluptuous being which indwells in the body of Homo sapien being attack a male being of Voluptuous being which indwells in the body of Homo sapien being ?"

"Yes. It would do. If a female Homo sapien being indwells in the body of Voluptuous being which is physically stronger than a male Homo sapien being indwells in the body of Voluptuous being which is physically weaker, then, that female being would attack this male being in copulation."

"Then, what would happen ?"

"Male being of Homo sapien who is actually Believer -in 'I' and has to ever be worshipped by Female being of Homo sapien who is actually Player-'I' would fall down from the status of accomplished or having actual to the lower or the lowest. At the same time, Female being of Homo sapien who am actually Player-'I' and have to ever worship Male being of Homo sapien would too fall down from the status of more accomplished or having actual more to the lowest at which it couldn't learn what it is, why it is in such and what it has to do. The being which couldn't learn what itself, why itself is as so and what itself has to do for itself is nothing but the Exploited being which has to die for another opportunity in forthcoming incarnation as there would be no other go for it even if it will breathe until its last breath. But it must not be expected to die before its natural last breath as long as if it doesn't continue to preclude the Practice of either Believer -in 'I' or Player-'I'."

"Can It assuredly get an opportunity in forthcoming incarnation ?"

"No certainty would be there. It can or It can not in forthcoming incarnation."

"Then, what ?"

"In any one of forthcoming incarnations it might get."

"In any one of forthcoming incarnations also there is not certainty. Only 'might'?"

"Yes. You are correct."

"Couldn't 'certainty' ever be possible ?"

"For 'certainty' possibility must be there."

"When ? In which incarnation ?"

"Certainty might not be possible in any of incarnation during present 'Many' exists. After termination of 'Will' of To be 'Many' of The Only "I", The Only "I" do 'Will' 'Not to be Many' termination of which again The Only "I" do will to be 'Many'. Thus 'To be Many' and 'Not to be Many' follow each other. In any one of 'To be Many', could get an opportunity assuredly."

"So, opportunity would be there !"

"Yes, opportunity would be there indubitably."

"Then, what is the Problem ?"

"Availability of exact sort of bodies."

"Why would such situation arise ?"

"When Homo sapien beings would abate their restraint or temperance or relinquish themselves to the bodily senses of each other without exerting their intellect having which is very peculiar to them."

"How could both they manage their temperance or themselves not to be relinquished to their bodily senses ?"

"In course of observing the Practice to regain the Unlost, a male being and a female being of Homo sapien whichever sorts they may be, must make efforts to do make loving in the course of copulating."

"When bodies of Homo sapien beings wouldn't contain sorts of their own in, how can they make efforts to do make loving ?"

"For any sort of being, indwelling in the body of Homo sapien is the grace of The Only "I". Because, a lot of scope would always be there for any sort to exert bodily senses like sort of Homo sapien does. By dint of bodily senses of Homo sapien both male and female sorts can talk to each other. Talking to each other as per their wish and choice is an untrained imparting which could originate themselves to be and do like Homo sapien beings."

"Being and doing like Homo sapien beings would endow what with them?"

"They would be endowed with art and skill of Making

Love to each other who would be led by each other to do intercourse."

"What is Making Love in real and what is Intercourse in True ?"

"Before them, You have to learn copulating."

Chapter-28

"Ah ! come on me."

"All along You behave as a libidinous being. Can't You keep Yourself not to be so for a while ?"

"Why should I be so ?"

"You are a Homo sapien being i.e. a human being like me."

"So what ?"

"I suppose You too have Mind like I do. I don't let You enjoy me."

"I suppose that the copulation between You and I executes both our Minds to delight in so that senses of us would get unknowledgeable of what are around us."

"But I can't believe in what You say at the same time I can't trust You."

"Why can't You trust me ?"

"I don't dare to believe You as You are fully libidinous even sultry."

"No, I am not at all a sultry; may be libidinous."

"Are You sure about Yourself ?"

"Sure. You can indubitably cooperate with me."

"Then, why are You late ?"

"Oh! You too have same feeling now."

"Not. As same as You do."

"It is clear You have feeling which may not be same level of me."

"That's right."

"At first I touch Your both shoulders with my palms. This touching must stir Your desire which isn't inclined to You as so."

"Then ! What is so ?"

"No doubt. It is a desire. My touching Your shoulders and Your touching mine suffice eyes of us to eye eyes of each other."

"What do Your eyes do mine."

"The Eyes are, at all times, the opened-doors, though they are closed in sleeping, which communicate all sorts of feelings."

"In this running second, what do Your eyes communicate and what do mine ?"

"At each and every second Your eyes and mine communicate such feelings which You and I have in that second."

"At this second, what feeling do You have ?"

"I have, at this second, such feeling which does arouse same feeling in You."

"Does Your feeling exhort mine ?"

"By all means."

"Come on. You can proceed."

"I am happy. I do come forward towards You and You too come forward towards me ."

"Yes. I have come as You have just asked. You too done."

"Now I am putting my palms on Your shoulders and rubbing them."

"Do I rub Yours ?"

"Yes. I am expecting You to do same in return."

"How are You feeling while I do as You expect ?"

"As I am already coveting; so I am relishing as I wish. What about You ?"

"I suppose Yours doing has just goaded me."

"Well. I think You can now instinctively relish."

"May be."

"I also think You feel a passion exactly which You may not tell."

"Yes. You are right. I am feeling a passion of which I can't tell."

"Now, come closer to me as both front sides of our bodies touch each other."

"When Your chest touched mine, I felt some rigour or trepidation."

"To get relief from that rigour or trepidation, I embrace You."

"It is hard. Please loose Your embracing."

"O.K. You also embrace me."

"Both fronts of our bodies are now almost appressed each other so that air couldn't pass through our fronts."

"Though we are so, we have to press our backs of each further close."

"Is it possible ?"

"We shall make it possible."

"O.K. Let us do."

"Now, what is happening to You ?"

"My breasts are getting crumpled."

"Can You endure crumpled breasts ?"

"I rejoice this. It seems that I am not enduring but rejoicing."

"Now Your rejoicing would call forth Your desire which is in hibernation."

"Yes. Now I am feeling something that may be longing."

"You are, so, feeling longing for something that can be appetency."

"How can I quench that appetency ?"

"I can make You quench by touching Your waist and pulling You more towards me."

"Owing to Your this pulling me, I feel my Vulva has just been struck by something."

"My penis has struck to Your Vulva ."

"As Your penis struck to my Vulva, I feel an odd experience. But I couldn't tell what is so ?"

"Till to You just felt odd experience, You have been a virgin physically."

"Mentally ?"

"In my view, You have already lost Your virginity mentally. But as I have observed no requital has been there yet. So You haven't lost Your virginity mentally."

"So, You can uphold that I am not a virgin physically."

"I can."

"How can You ?"

"So because, You have just Yourself told that You felt an odd experience."

"So what !"

"Without applying one's mind, one couldn't feel experience."

"So, You have adjudged that I applied my mind."

"Both Your Vulva and my Penis are of genital organs. Only the Mind could control them not to be reacted when they are touched each other. In present situation I am applying my mind. So I had pulled You towards me and got succeeded in striking my Penis to Your Vulva whereas it is clear You did not apply Your mind to let Your Vulva struck by my Penis. Therefore You have not lost Your virginity mentally. But You told that You had felt an odd experience. So....."

"So..."

"So, without minding experience can't be possible. But Your Vulva is an upper part of Your genital organ. My Penis is my genital organ. When both touch each other, whimsical agitation i.e. a kind of disturbance can instinctively be occurred. Hence, this occurrence can not be an experience in true."

"When I have not lost my virginity mentally, how will You uphold me ?"

"Upto Your Vulva struck by my Penis, You lost one by third of Your score of advantageousness in this doing which would be accounted for Your forthcoming incarnations."

"Can I achieve so what I lost ?"

"You can. But it couldn't be possible to learn that whether You can achieve what You lost only in present incarnation or in forthcoming incarnations."

"How can You tell that I can achieve again what I lost ?"

"Actually You have lost nothing. I too haven't lost anything. It is the Illusion that both we have lost the thing to regain which we are striving for from time immemorial."

"How can this Illusion can be dissipated ?"

"In course of the Practice meant to regain the Unlost."

"What You are doing to me and making me do as You wish is the part of Practice You observe."

"This the question of trillions of trillion dollars. Actually I am doing what to You is not my wish but my concupiscence."

"Why haven't You felt the wish to do me so ?"

"Owing to cherish Illusion that physical sexual enjoyment is only genuine enjoyment, I have just deemed that concupiscence is to be acceptable. Under impact of same Illusion, now, I keep my stretched palms on Your both buttocks and thrust them against me while kneading both."

"As You doing so, I sense Your penis that struck my Vulva is getting erected more and more."

"Can You find difference between feel and sense ?"

"I can. But I can't answer exactly."

"The sense is that something which body experiences whereas feel is that an understanding of something."

"But I uttered the word 'sense' spontaneously."

"So, You haven't lost virginity mentally."

"If I haven't lost so yet, what will You be going to do further."

"Now, I kiss Your both lips with my lips."

"Your kissing propelling me towards You to let You do what You want."

"Aren't You enjoying my kissing Your lips ?"

"Isn't my propelling my enjoying Your kissing ?"

"I may suppose Your propelling is as Your enjoying my kissing Your lips. As You told, I too agree with You that You are propelling but not enjoying."

"How can You determine ?"

"If You have enjoyed, You would have closed Your eyes which speak out what You couldn't have spoken out in enjoying."

"You are right. I have not closed my eyes when You were kissing my lips. But, in spite of my eyes were open, I could not watch all our surroundings."

"Yes. You couldn't watch. But You must have seen them.

"Yes. I have seen."

"You could have seen all which You couldn't have watched. Because, during my kissing all Your brains have been stopped to function. When the functioning of brains is not done no enjoyment will be experienced."

"So what !"

"So, You have been still a virgin mentally at all."

"Then, what are You going to do hereafter ?"

"I am going to hug You from Your back so that. I can cup Your breasts with my stretched palms."

"I am feeling that Your erected penis is trying to enter the interval where my both buttocks join together and make tickled me."

"Have You felt tickling only ?"

"As You touched some parts of my body, I feel that my body is urging from You something what is it I can't tell You."

"So, the state of Your body is, now, not like it was just before."

"It may be."

"So, there is no exception for me to lick Your Vulva and Vagina."

"Doing so is a thing of supposition ?"

"Why do You think like that ?"

"Even to imagine, that is untoward. Isn't that ?"

"That is not. In copulation it is accepted as fun."

"If it is acceptable as You said, I shall let You do so."

"Lie over on the bed while turning on the back and spread Your legs as wide as possible."

"Oh! hh! Wooo! I feel Your tongue is encircling inside me. Isn't it ?"

"Yes. It is. Let me continue so for a while."

"Still for a long ! I can't sustain that tickling aroused by encircling of Your tongue for even a little long."

"Are You feeling pain or annoyance of tickling aroused ?

"It is neither a pain nor an annoyance."

"Can't You enjoy encircling of my tongue inside You ?"

"It is not enjoying too. But I feel it is a thing of unwanting and is to be ashamed."

"Why do You deem it to be ashamed ?"

"Now what You have just done is sordid and vile."

"But I did it."

"Without making my mind up, I let You do so."

"So, You are still a virgin mentally. It's o.k. Let me make my utmost effort."

"What is it ?"

"To insert my erected penis into Your vagina."

"No, don't do that."

"Why ?"

"It is nothing but abysmal and despicable."

"Without inserting erected penis into Vagina, the seduction couldn't be consummated."

"It is a seduction what You are attempting since a long ? why do You do it to me ?"

"As a male I have to do to You and as a female You have to be done, then only, thoroughness is accumulated to our incarnations done due to our separation of each from The Only "I"."

"What is the thoroughness to be accumulated ?"

"Thoroughness is in two kinds."

"What are they ?"

"To let an each and every 'I' go to indwell in the body formed in Your body due to either copulation or Love Making or intercourse and to be begotten is an instant thoroughness. Another is to lose the consciousness of the body whether it is functioning."

"If so, why are You late ? carry on."

Chapter-29

"Amazing ! Very next day only You Yourself have started to kissing me."

"Why are You Amazing ! You Yourself have allured me to taste of seduction."

"Have You recollected what I did to You Yesterday ?"

"I have not done."

"Then, how can You have Yourself come forward to seduce me ?"

"All parts of my body which You riled have just compelled me to be nymphomanical ?"

"What is happening to You as You are nymphomanical ?"

"The parts or organs of my body which were struck, rubbed, goaded, touched, were appressed, pressed, crumpled, thrusted, kneaded, propelled and tickled etc. by Your doing so and so have been very prurient now."

"Why so ? I can't understand. Even I can't subside them. Without my intention, they are eagerly demanding same intense gratification."

"Are You sure that You have not intended to kiss me ?"

"Yes. I am sure."

"Have You tried to control or dominate or manage parts or organs of Your body not to be prurient ?"

"Even I have not supposed to do so. Instinctively I have started to kissing You."

"So, without making Your intent efforts, You have started to kissing me."

"Yes. I have."

"When my penis was inserted into Your Vagina, almost You screamed. Why did You do so ?"

"At that time, I felt some extent heavy pain and inexplicable surprise."

"Even for least extent, didn't You enjoy inserting my penis ?"

"As far as my bethinking, I didn't enjoy."

"I let my penis wobble in Your Vagina instead of playing while giving strokes. If I did so, You might have enjoyed."

"If You did so, what would have been happened to me."

"You might have surely enjoyed a lot."

"Then, why didn't You do so to me accordingly ?"

"As You were a virgin mentally, You were very tight so that You screamed and I didn't dare to outdo."

"Why were I tight ? When can I be penetrable ?"

"As long as You are a virgin mentally, You can not be easily or facilely penetrable."

"How am I deprived of my mental virginity ?"

"When You will be the enabler to translate what You feel physically into mental-enjoyment simultaneously, then only, You can be deprived of Your mental virginity."

"Do I need deprivation of my mental virginity ?"

"Yes. You need. You are now a Ritualistic being. I am too same being. The Ritualistic beings are those which can regain what they have, in true, Unlost and could regain by dint of Love Making too."

"Love Making ! What is it ?"

"When You would take part in copulation physically and mentally in equal proportion with Your co-partner, then, Love Making can be done to both You and Your partner."

"Can't I take part in such copulation ?"

"At present You can't. Even I too can't."

"You too ! How that ?"

"Yesterday, I seduced You only."

"Didn't You love make to me on Your part ?"

"It couldn't have been possible to me. Not only to me, none

could have made love to You. At present, in lieu of me, none could make love to You."

"Why ?"

"Love Making can be possible when both partners would love each other, respect each other and honour each other in equal and in same manner."

"Only with loving each other, couldn't it be possible ?"

"Loving some is a virtue graced by The Only "I" of whose bits are each and every 'I', but You may not love each and every one but You must not keep Yourself not to love any one of each and every 'I'. So, Loving some only is not adequate. Besides, loving some can't be possible as You suppose to love some. Love must be emanated naturally without supposing. Inexplicably, Love contains desire or ambition. Even Love can expect same from those to whom it emanates. One who loves another one ever deems that another one must be of One only not of some other else. In such situation, One naturally doesn't let another one, whom one loves, prefer to some other else in anything. This sort of unletting affects to honour or respect others. Therefore only with loving each other, Love Making couldn't be possible."

"Along with loving, if each other does respect, then ?"

"When You feel that You should admire someone for one's goodness in something or someone should be treated in an appropriate way, then, You would respect that someone. You can respect others too alike. So, Loving and respecting aren't too adequate."

"Along with loving and respecting, if each other do honour, then ?"

"When You feel that You must regard someone whose worth You would esteem without second thought, then, You would honour that someone. Like that both Ritualistic beings, if love each other, respect each other and honour each other in equal proportion while ignoring all sorts of distinction regarding age, colour, status, etc. can make love to each other. But pertaining to age male Ritualistic being i.e. Believer-in 'I' must be older.

"Why should Believer-in 'I' be older than Player -'I'."

"You have already known that the level or the range of cherishing the Illusion in 'Being' of each and every 'I' is less than in 'Doing' of each and every 'I' would be male-being. If the level or the range of cherishing is vice-versa, then, each and every 'I' would be female-being. So, in Beingness, Believer-in 'I' i.e. male-being is older than Player-'I' i.e. female-being. So only, the female Ritualistic being must select the male Ritualistic being which is older in age."

"If so, in Your view Love Making can be possible between You and I."

"Can not be possible."

"Then, why did You attempt to seduce me and succeed in it ?"

"I couldn't have controlled myself when You have cast Your amorous looking at me."

"Why couldn't You have ?"

"As I have immersed in Illusion in such level in which I couldn't have controlled."

"If so You have, what will be happened to You ?"

"Already something happened to me."

"What is that something ?"

"As a Believer-in 'I' or a Ritualistic-being, I could have been not to be attracted or affected by any such as Your amorous looking."
"Have You been attracted or affected by my amorous looking ?"

"Yes."

"What will You do or will be done to You ?"

"I have just seduced to You and am going to be seduced by You."

Chapter-30

"Actually I would have kept myself to be a Ritualistic being without seducing You or myself being seduced by You."

"You mean both we are seducers."

"Yes. Owing to be affected by Your amorousness extended towards me, I, at first. seduced You. Later on You have done same to me in return."

"What You did to me earlier, in Your view, might be seducing to me. But, is that, which I did to You in return later, too seducing ?"
"Yes."

"How that ?"

"What I had done to You was done under impact of Your amorousness. Even my 'instinction' warned me not to behave with You alike and not to defile Your body and deflower You. But I paid little attention to listen to the warning."

"When under impact of my amorousness You behaved with me alike, how would I have been seduced by You?"

"This is the question to which answer is hardly possible. In the ripening period, a Player -'I' must be coached to behave with a Believer-in 'I' not to be affected. Physical body is that which can be easily accustomed to opposite physical body in sex. So, Your physical body made You cast amorous looking at me."

"So, the shortcoming which provoked me to cast amorous looking at You is with my physical body but not myself."
"With Yourself only."

"How ?"

"Your 'Mind' is there. Your 'Intellect' is also there. Your 'Mind' must have applied Your 'Intellect'."

"But, how couldn't I have applied ?"

"Your body, then, overpowered Your 'Mind' so that Your 'Mind' couldn't have applied 'Intellect."

"When my body overpowered my 'Mind' and my 'Mind' consequently couldn't have applied 'Intellect', then, how can wrong be with me."
"Because, You are not a Voluptuous being but a Homo sapien being. Hence, a Homo sapien being is ever expected to be alert at each and every second to apply the Mind as Homo sapien being stands for the Mind with the Intellect not for the senses without the 'Sense'."

"When along with all Voluptuous beings, Homo sapien beings are also graced with sexual organs and sexual desires to be quenched, What is wrong with either a Player-'I' or a Believer-in 'I' to quench so as per its choice."

"Nothing would be with either."

"Then."

"Then, both that Player-'I' and Believer-in 'I' must lose their Homo sapien beingness in forthcoming incarnations. This would be too a falling down not from the Absoluteness of The Only "I" but from the Homo sapienness which might be from the beginning i.e. from the starting of 'Will' to be 'Many' done by The Only "I"."

"Then, what will happen ?"

"Either from incarnations to incarnations during single 'Many' come into existence by the 'Will' of The Only "I" or many of 'Many' to many of 'Many' being come into existence respectively after a 'Not to be Many' and another Not to be 'Many', You would have to go on as a Voluptuous being until You regain what You unlost in true."

"Oh! How horrible it is ! How have I uttered the word 'horrible' without my Knowledge ? Even I don't know whether I have uttered the word in the appropriate context or not ?"

"You might not have Knowledge of Your uttering. Even You don't have exact context for the word to be uttered. But both You and I would be the forms of 'KNOWLEDGE'."

"Forms of Knowledge ! Is the Knowledge a thing of Matter i.e. of 'Many'?

"KNOWLEDGE is neither a thing nor a being nor any item of the Matter but It is the form of The Only "I".

"When It is the Form of The Only "I", how could The Only

"I" be said that The Only "I" am beyond one who is called to have Knowledge ?"

"Not only the KNOWLEDGE, the IDEOLOGY is also a form of The Only "I". But the Ideology can be assumed into a shape in the brain of human being who is knower of something or some other thing. When a thing is known and when a knower can assume that known thing into a shape, then, The Only "I" am beyond those Knowledge and ideology which are, notwithstanding, forms of The Only "I"."

"When both the Knowledge and the Ideology are the forms of The Only "I", why would The Only "I" be beyond them ?"

"Whatever and whichever it or they may be, whenever or wherever it or they can be perceptible to the beings in the 'Many', that it or that they would be kept as limited all in all, so, The Only "I", who am unlimited in any, would be beyond that it or that they."

"So, The Only "I" would be beyond both You and I."

"Yes."

"So, You can endorse that I uttered the word, 'Horrible' with my Knowledge."

"Yes. You did but without learning the word, 'Horrible'."

"Learning ?"

"Yes. Learning. The Ultimate Thing is to be known is The Only "I". To know that Thing, each and every 'I', at first, know that each and every 'I' am only That Thing. When each and every 'I' can know each and every 'I' am only That Thing, then, each and every must learn That Thing."

"How can each and every 'I' learn That Thing ?"

"Doing the Practice is only the Learning."

"When would the Learning be possible ?"

"At all times. Because, though each and every 'I' am not clear that each and every 'I' am a knower, each and every 'I' am indubitably a knower. But every each and every 'I' may not be aware of that every each and very 'I' am a knower. Likewise You haven't been aware of that You are a knower. But You are a knower. So only, You uttered the word 'horrible'. Thus You are a knower of everything. By Learning i.e. doing the Practice You can learn that You are only the Knowledge."

"When I learn that I am a knower or the Knowledge, what will happen to me ?"

"Who oneself learns that oneself is the knower, then, that one would withstand oneself as a knower and do, act and behave accordingly."

Chapter-31

"When could You make love to me instead of doing copulation or seducing ?"

"When You would lose Your virginity mentally while I seduce You or You seduce me, I might make love to You."

"Wouldn't I lose mine in either situation ?"

"Do You love me sincerely ?"

"I suppose I do."

"But in our either seductions, I haven't found love in You with me."

"Did I cooperate with You without love with You ?"

"Even You didn't react what I had done to You."

"Then, what did I do ?"

"You did nothing. Your sexual organs had responded according to my doing."

"What about seduction which I did to You ?"

"During Your seduction being done to me, only Your sexual organs avenged my sexual organs."

"But I supposed that I had seduced You as You had done."

"Yes. You seduced. But with Your sexual organs."

"I too rubbed, stuck, touched even sucked You in my way. Didn't 'I'?"

"Yes. You did all which You told. Even Voluptuous beings would also do what we did to each other."

"Weren't Your organs quenched when I seduced You."

"Yes. My organs which You seduced were quenched."

"Then, why aren't You satisfied ?"

"While You were seducing me, I couldn't have been wrapped up in that doing."

"How could You uphold that You couldn't have been ?"

"Not only myself You couldn't too have been wrapped up in my seduction being done to You."

"How could You have deduced that I couldn't too have wrapped up in ?"

"Because, You were brooding over my seducing. Weren't You ?"

"Yes. I was. How could You have made out that You too couldn't have wrapped up in ?"

"At first I amazed when You had started to kissing me which I hadn't imagined."

"You might have amazed ! So what ?"

"My amazing made me idle. Like Your organs did when I seduced, my organ did."

"Actually what I had to do in return when You seduced me and what You had to do when I did to You ?"

"You had to go into ecstasy when I seduced to You and I had to go into it when You did to me."

"In which duration, I mean in the beginning, in the middle and in the end of seduction ?"

"At each and every step of seducing."

"How ?"

"Either in Copulation or in Love Making Homo sapien beings or Ritualistic beings, it can be upheld that the 'KISS' would be the very first step which couldn't be taken by Voluptuous beings."

"What is the 'KISS' ?"

"Listen carefully. I narrate it in poetic manner. When 'KISS' is given and taken, both feel that

All functions of All
Could be stopped.

No outcome of any
Can be missed at all.

If it so happened, it
Can't be a hindrance.

If it isn't appeared, it
Can't be a pitfall.

If it isn't listened, it
Can't be the fetters.

If it isn't touched, it
Can't be discrepancy.

If it isn't struck, it
Can't be the inertia.

If it isn't moved, it
Can't be the stasis.

If it isn't aware of, it
Can't be concerned."

"You mean both of us had to fall in this situation during our each seduction."

"Yes. You have correctly understood."

"Now, Some extent I can understand what You mean. But how can this be possible ?"

"When as a female being You can view me not only as a male being but as a bestower of the spirit of Love, then, You would go into ecstasy. When You submit Yourself to me while viewing me alike, I would have to be as such bestower. Then only both our Minds get overpowered our bodies though our organs behave according to our instincts. Then only, this can be possible."

"Could I view You as a bestower of the spirit of Love ?"

"You can snatch answer to this question not from me as it can be available within Yourself."

"You mean 'viewing is mine'."

"Yes."

"If I find the answer that You don't deserve to be viewed alike, then…,"

"Now You have perfectly come on the way. Until You find such male Homo sapien being or Ritualistic being, You ought not to behave with any while looking at amorously etc."

"If I behave like as You told, could I find You on any point of time as my bestower of the spirit of Love ?"

"You could fancy me as Your bestower. But it is the matter of my 'instinct'."

Chapter-32

"If both of us carry on seducing to each other consistently as possible as to us, couldn't You prove to be bestower of me and myself as donee of Your bestowing ?"

" 'Seducing' consistently would hold us to be either lewd or libidinous or sultry or libido or lustful etc. but not devoted to each other and no courtship between us developed."

"Being devoted to each other is a must."

"Earlier to it, both of us must develop courtship between us."

"Let us make efforts develop so."

"Not possible. The Doors are closed."

"How?"

"You had to translate Your amorousness cast towards me as courtship and expect same from me."

"Let us endeavour with our best to develop courtship."

"The association of deed done physically or mentally or physically and mentally must be adhered to the Mind i.e. macro Form of the Atman (the Soul) which would be in the form of Casual body that would have been there while 'Not to be Many' would last as per the 'Will' done by The Only "I". The association, which would emanate due to only physical deed in Homo sapien being or Ritualistic being, could not be blown over."

"Even during next incarnation too, couldn't it be ?"

"It can't exactly be told that during the next incarnation it could be done. If we take birth as Homo sapien beings in any of forthcoming incarnations, maybe, it could be done."

"Could any association be blown over in forthcoming incarnation or incarnations ?"

"Not each and every association could be done. If we stop seducing each other hence forward and carry on deeds while applying the Mind, then, this association would be very weak in forthcoming incarnation or any one of incarnations. When this association would be weak in comparison with other associations, lot of scope must be there for this association to be blown over during 'The Present Many' only."

"Could we keep this in our memory in forthcoming incarnation or incarnations ?"

"We couldn't keep it at any cost."

"Why ?"

"Because, Forgetfulness is the Grace of The Only "I" in this regard. If Homo sapien being is graced to memorize and recollect any association emanated in the previous incarnation or incarnations, that association would affect again and again or time and again the deed or deeds which are being done in the current incarnation."

"You mean none of associations could be memorized or recollected ?"

"There You are."

"When we couldn't memorize or recollect anyone of associations, from where we would have to resume our Practice ?"

"Taking all associations emanated due to either auspicious deeds or sinister deeds or assorted deeds into account, each and every 'I' would opt a body of Homo sapien being prepared in a particular Lineage to indwell in. The Lineage is the first and foremost dignity which would provide so many relations, confinements, bindings, knots, affinities, alliances, kinship, rapport, conditions, clauses, appetences even wedlocks etc. Those, who could act as guides to the Lineage, must impart for what the Lineage stands and its decency, dignity and obligations to all growing in that Lineage to be promoted as incumbents."

"If no guides are there in certain Lineage, then, ?"

"Unavailability of guides in a Lineage is also a consequence of associations emanated in previous incarnation or incarnations of those who entered into that Lineage. So, any or few or many each and every 'I' who entered into that Lineage must research possible things pertaining to the genealogy of that Lineage and study them to improve the Lineage. If no such research is done by those who are indwelling in the bodies of Homo sapien and have taken birth in that Lineage in that contemporary period, the associations emanated for the research is undone would be adhered to them."

"How could things of the Lineage help for sexual relationship between a male Homo sapien and a female Homo sapien being ?"

"Both male Homo sapien being and female Homo sapien

being can learn what is auspicious deed and what is sinister deed. If they themselves habituate to attend auspicious deeds, it would be the Practice meant to regain the Unlost."

"What are the auspicious deeds ?"

"Auspicious deed would be so doing of which the doer must not be affected by the sensuous desires and any other must not be done by same too."

"If they attend sinister deeds....?"

"It would be the Undoing of them. They would have to go on in 'Many' after 'Many' while entering into a body of a sort and exiting it to enter into a body of another sort. This going on can be done through out many of 'Not to be Many' and 'to be Many' being done by the 'Will' of The Only "I"."

"If they attend assorted deeds....?"

"Their Practice must be affected. Hence, they would be graced with required capability to commence their Practice and forego their gained capability in attending auspicious deeds. Thus, their Practice must be fluctuated. So, scope is for them to reincarnate in different sorts again and again in the current 'Many' but no scope is for them to regain the Unlost in this 'Many' only."

"Oh ! But I have put question regarding sexual relationship. Haven't I ?"

"Sexual relationship is an item in the subject of the Lineage."

"What is it ?"

"No Lineage, in view of kinship, would allow sexual relationship between a male and a female who would be from itself. The Lineage would transmit all its own established decency, dignity and obligation to all its male beings and female beings. Owing to such transmission all male beings and female beings can be either impressed or influenced or inspired or inculcated or fascinated by the established."

Chapter-33

"Can these transmitted established values check and control all male and female beings ?"

"No, certainty would not be there."

"How ?"

"No certainty is there for Homo sapien beings to be free from any quantity of beastlihoodness_of which Voluptuous beings would exist."

"How would they be with beastlihoodness ?"

"Owing to their associations emanated from either sinister deeds or assorted deeds done in previous incarnation or incarnations in Present 'Many' or Earlier 'Many' to Present 'Many'."

" How could they get free from so ?"

"So only, all Homo sapien beings must be, with intensity, indoctrinated all the auspiciousness in all activities undertaken by the Lineage. This indoctrinated- auspiciousness would de-escalate beastlihoodness at least in the least quantity and quality which may enable Homo sapien beings to behave as Homo sapien beings who could only befit Ritualistic beings."

"Is there any possibility for any Homo sapien being to be free from entire beastlihoodness in the Lineage ?"

"There may be either possibility or impossibility for any

Homo sapien being."

"If there is possibility for a Homo sapien being in a Lineage…?"

"That would be an advantage to such Lineage to get at least all its own Homo sapien beings transformed into Ritualistic beings who can work on all other Homo sapien beings from other Lineages."

"If there is no possibility..?"

"They would have to go on as Voluptuous beings while indwelling in the bodies of Homo sapien."

"So, it is hardly possible to evaluate which Homo sapien being is free from beastlihoodness in toto ?"

"Yes. There You are."

"What must Homo sapien do to do, act or behave like Homo sapien ?"

"At first Homo sapien must know its own Lineage. Later on, learn that it must not suppose even in dreams to have illicit affairs with any Homo sapien being from its Lineage and behave with all from its Lineage as its children or parents. The Parent is expected not to beget progeny only but also get its progeny flourished physically, mentally and spiritually. The child is expected not only to perpetuate its Lineage but perpetuate the spiritual values established by its Parent and grand Parent even great grand Parent."

"How could these values bear arms ?"

"These values check all illicit affairs among beings from same Lineage. Later on, if the beings are indoctrinated spiritually, they either opt or select their better-haves from other Lineages."

"Can option or selection be given the green light to both male Homo sapien being and female Homo sapien ?"

"No, only The Player-'I' i.e. female Homo sapien being from a Lineage can be given the green light to opt or select male Homo sapien being from another Lineage."

"When can a female Homo sapien being from a Lineage be given green light to opt ?"

"When there are two or very few male Homo sapien beings from different Lineages or a Lineage other than of female Homo sapien, then, female Homo sapien would opt a male Homo sapien being. Here it is ever to be noted that the female Homo sapien being would have to opt a male Homo Spien being from those who are endorsed by the Lineage of that female Homo sapien."

"When can a female Homo sapien being be given green light to select a male Homo sapien being ?"

"When there are so many male Homo sapien beings from various Lineages of same 'clan' other than of female Homo sapien being, then, that female Homo sapien being can be given green light to select its own choice."

"What is the 'Clan' ?"

"The 'clan' is a group of Lineages. It is a categorization of its people into groups based on factors like occupation which would offer services to all those whose occupations are varied. As such categorization is the position of the 'Clan'. This 'Clan' can be called as caste etc. Each and every 'Clan' adopt its own way of living, traditions and customs etc. The traditions and customs are only its own constitutions. As per its own constitution, the 'Clan' never accepts or approves or allows inter-clan wedding."

"Can male Homo sapien being never be given green light to opt or select a female Homo sapien being ?"

"Never."

"Why ?"

"Each and every male Homo sapien being is at all events a Believer-in 'I'. It must believe in itself that it would be The Only "I" who would do 'Will' to be 'Many' and 'Not to be Many' respectively. Like The Only "I", It must upkeep itself not to be fallen from Its 'Beingness'."

"What is the Beingness ?"

"The Only "I" would ever be The Only "I", because The Only "I" would never Condescend or Descend from The Only "I" into 'The Many' which would come into existence due to the 'Will' of The Only "I". The Only "I" would eternally be beyond that 'Many' though that 'Many' would not be other then The Only "I". So, the 'Beingness' of The Only "I" could not be affected. Likewise, each and every male Homo sapien being must not fall into mundane pleasures which affect Beingness of It."

"What will happen, if 'Beingness' is affected ?"

"Though that male Homo sapien being is a Believer-in 'I', it would have to behave, in 'Spiritual sense', as a Player-'I'."

"Then what will happen ?"

"It would have to do the Practice to know and learn the Belief in itself."

"Can't It do the Practice straightly as the Player-'I' ?"

"Never, It couldn't."

Chapter-34

"Are both a Player-'I' and a Believer-in 'I' differed from each other in sex and the spirit too ?"

"Yes. But regarding the Spirit i.e. the Atman (the Soul), there would be difference in the Spiritual sense."

"Are there two Spiritualities ?"

"The 'Spirituality' is only One. No second Spirituality would ever be there."

"Actually what is the Spiritual sense ?"

"In other way this item was already discussed. However, let me tell You once again."

" The Supreme spirit or only One spirit or the Atman (the Soul) would only be there. Except the Supreme spirit, Nothing or Nobody would be there. This Supreme spirit would be only The Only "I". This Supreme spirit or The Only "I" would be beyond even 'Beingness' and 'Doingness' too. When The Only "I" do 'Will' to be 'Many', then only, the terms of 'Beingness' and 'Doingness' are at first introduced. During 'the Many', except The Only "I", all the things and the beings would be more than one in each. So only, The "I" would be qualified with the word, 'Only'. Each and every 'I' am actually One i.e. Only "I" but during the 'Many' each and every 'I' am too looked as fascinated as there are so many of each and every 'I'. Though each and every 'I' am only The Only "I" or the Supreme spirit, when each and every 'I' would be fascinated as Many during the 'Many', then, the Spirituality of each and every 'I' who am the Supreme spirit would be Many i.e. in two between them One would stand for the 'Beingness' and another for the 'Doingness'."

" Who stands for the Beingness and who stands for the Doingness ?"

"The Believer-in 'I' stand for the Beingness and The Player-'I' for the Doingness."

"Standing for the Beingness means what ?"

"The Believer-in 'I' must not fall for carnal desires. When The Player-'I' very conscientiously devote itself to The Believer-in 'I' in course of the Practice meant to regain the Unlost, then only, The Believer-in 'I' can grace The Player-'I'."

"Why is The Player-'I' only commanded to devote itself to The Believer-in 'I' ?"

" The Player-'I' is graced with the onus to develop a new individual when its own fertilized by the sperm of male and let grow that individual into a body in which an each and every 'I' indwell to resume the Practice which had taken a pause in previous incarnation or another each and every 'I' which had been in the body of Voluptuous being and was qualified to enter into the body of Homo sapien being."

"Why isn't the Believer-in 'I' commanded to grace itself upon the Player-'I' ?"

"The Onus to develop bodies by the grace of The Believer-in 'I' is kept on the shoulders of The Player-'I'. When The Player-'I' devotes Herself to the Believer-in 'I', then only, the Believer-in 'I' am commanded to grace. Otherwise the Believer-in 'I' keep Himself not to be fallen off."

"When The Believer-in 'I' grace upon the Player-'I', isn't gracing fallen off ?"

"Gracing The Devotee is neither falling off nor quenching carnal desires and not a doing on part of The Believer-in 'I' at all ?"

"How? In the gracing of The Believer-in 'I', don't sexual organs of The Believer-in 'I' participate ?"

"Surely. Participation of sexual organs of The Believer-in 'I' is only the gracing."

"When sexual organs of The Believer-in 'I' participate, aren't sexual organs of The Believer-in 'I' got quenched regarding carnal desires ?"

"When there are the devotion of The Player-'I' towards The Believer-in 'I' and the gracing of The Believer-in 'I' upon The Player -'I', then, there won't be ugliness means a transition from the benignant state of the Mind."

"Doesn't ugliness mean unpleasantness or offensiveness ?"

"Literally, ugliness means unpleasantness. In the present context, affecting the Mind while devoting and gracing are being done."

"How can the affecting be done ?"

"At present I can narrate it in poetic manner."

My hands cover Your back.
I press You against me.
You do same as I.
Both our fronts touch closely,
Little air can pass through.
I see my image in Your
Eyes, You do same in mine.
Both we can't speak out
As my lips shut Yours.
Your and my ears hear only
Our passionate breathing sounds.
We don't listen to a breeze
That too can't cool our bodies.
All of our senses heed
Nothing except to drink in.
Nerves under our skins fail.
To communicate any message.
You submit all of Yours;
I too do same as You.
Unique tastes of both of us
Get lost their uniqueness.
We each other touch and press
Each and soft parts of bodies.
Both our brains are alike;
They can't perform as they can.
Both we forget all agonies
And get peace as we wish.
Except none, we are to each.
Nothing or none can uncouple us.
All ours bless our insensibility.
I see none in You ever;
I am sure You do as I.

Both we are of the opinion that
A thought of Your comparison
Of me and my of You with others
Unsanctifies, Poisons and Mars
Cause of our each sub-mission.

Though in this state too, The Believer-in 'I' am not in absolute state to grace The Player-'I'. For the gracing of The Believer-in 'I' upon The Player-'I', no affecting can be there."

"How can You tell, it is not the absolute state?"

"Take down on Your Mind the line of poem just read which reads 'Cause of our each sub-mission'. In this line there are two words one is 'Cause' and another one is 'Submission'."

"So what ?"

"No doubt there is a 'Cause' for submission of the Player-'I' to the Believer-in 'I'. But for The Believer-in 'I', there is the 'Cause' only even The Believer-in 'I' Myself is the cause for the Doings of the Practice meant to regain the Unlost."

"What is wrong with The Believer-in 'I' to submit to The Player-'I' ?"

"Exclusively The Believer-in 'I' must believe in The Only "I" only. Actually Believing is not at all playing a role or doing a deed but Being as the Believer-in 'I' around the clock without losing refrainment."
"Regarding The Player-'I', is there exception for believing-in?"
"The Player-'I' would always be commanded to believe in The Believer-in 'I' whom The Player-'I' opts or selects as per My choice."

"Isn't it a discrimination observed by The Only "I" or being observed by The Believer-in 'I' ?"

"No, it isn't. The Only "I" would ever be free from all omissions and commissions even The Only "I" would be beyond all of 'The Many' whatever they may be. This observation is of both The Believer-in 'I' and The Player-'I'."

"Why so are they?"

"When The Believer-in 'I' and The Player-'I' have themselves lost their absoluteness due to their cherishing the Illusion that they are not The Only "I" but each and every 'I' am in consequence of the 'Will' done by The Only "I", the observing of this discrimination is existing in both The Player-'I' and The Believer-in 'I' from time immemorial i.e. beginning of 'The Many'."

"Couldn't this discrimination be expunged ?"

"Couldn't be done."

"Why ?"

"Because, this Discrimination is not appertaining to the bodies in which each and every 'I' indwell or to the Mind i.e. Macro form of the Atman (the Soul) of each and every 'I' but to the Atman (the Soul) straight away."

Chapter-35

"The Atman (the Soul) of The Believer-in 'l' and The Atman (the Soul) of The Player-'I' are differed from each other ?"

"No, Never. Both would ever be one and the same. Even the word 'both' couldn't be applicable here."

"But You have just told that the discrimination is to the Atman (the Soul)."

"In true, The Only "I" would be only there. When The Only "I" do 'Will' to be 'Many', This 'Many' would be in two. One is the Matter i.e. five elements and Another One am each and every 'l'. This each and every 'l' am too Many in number i.e. there are more each and every 'l' than one. All of each and every 'l' are in two groups. One group is of The Believer-in 'l' who stand for 'Beingness' and Another one group is of The Player-'I' who stand for 'Doingness'. Thus in standing for only both are differed from each other but not characteristically."

"Why would the Atman (the Soul) would be so i.e. differing from each other in standing for ?"

"In 'the Many' come into existence due to 'Will' done by The Only "I", either the Matter i.e. five elements or the Atman (the Soul) i.e. each and every 'l' could not be unique. The Only "I" would only be the Unique."

"Why would an each and every 'l' be as The Believer-in 'l' and another each and every 'I' be as The Player-'I'. Why shouldn't earlier one be as later as earlier ?"

"Beingness of an each and every 'I' and Doingness of another each and every 'I' would be established simultaneously while one and another one cherishing the Illusion. If it is told in crystal clear, the cherishing of the Illusion would establish who am for Beingness and who for Doingness."

"Can The Believer-in 'I' be transformed into The Player-'I' in any incarnation ?"

"Couldn't be done alike. Not only in any incarnation but in any 'Many' too."

"How long they would go on as so and so ?"

"Until they regain what they haven't lost, they would go on."

"Can't their physical bodies be too transformed into each other ?"

"By dint of 'Intellect' graced upon Homo sapien beings, the Homo sapien beings can change their bodies i.e. physical body of male being and physical body of female being into each other. But The casual bodies of male and female Homo sapien beings couldn't be transformed into each other."

"If a male being of Homo sapien gets changed its physical body into physical body of female being by dint of 'Intellect', then....?"

"By means of changed physical body, that Homo sapien being can quench its carnal desires."

"Isn't quenching carnal desires adequate ?"

"Each and every body of being i.e. Voluptuous being or Homo sapien being or Ritualistic being is not a physical body only but mental body and spiritual body also. So, quenching carnal desires is not adequate."

"Can't quenching carnal desires facilitate mental body and spiritual body to get any of them propitiate ?"

"Never. Mental body i.e. the Mind of a Homo sapien being is to be adhered to the associations emanated from the deeds done. A Homo sapien being is expected to attend any deed when its Mind apply its 'Intellect'. For a Homo sapien being, 'Intellect' is graced to be applied for the being to march forward to regain the Unlost. The casual body of a being would ever keep all commensurable associations adhered to the Mind i.e. Macro form of the Atman (the Soul) and grace that being accordingly whenever that being re-entered into the 'Many' which would come into existence after elapsing of 'Not to be Many' which would follow the previous 'Many'. In such course, the association emanated due to getting its physical body, that being must undergo without exerting acquired body (physical) whether it may be of male or female at least for a long in the next 'Many'."

"For that being wouldn't incarnation or incarnations be there ?"

"Incarnation or incarnations must be there. But during the forthcoming incarnation or incarnations it would be a Voluptuous being. Because, that being has addicted to carnal desires without applying the Mind like Voluptuous being in the Present incarnation."

"If it undergoes exerting acquired physical body alike, what will happen ?"

"Owing to its previous associations which were emanated from some of auspicious deeds, that being if takes incarnation as a male being of Homo sapien, it wouldn't grace female being i.e. it would be as an impotent to participate in copulation or if takes as a female being it wouldn't be a donee of bestowing of any male Homo sapien being."

Chapter-36

"Submission of the Player-'I' means what ?"

"Submission means, here, accepting The Believer-in 'I' as the Authority over The Player-'I'. Spiritually The Player-'I' have accepted the Authority of The Believer-in 'I' over The Player-'I'."

"Physically and in Mentally…?"

"Too."

"You mean, Can a male Homo sapien being exercise its authority over a female Homo sapien ?"

"Recollect what I have just told that The Player-'I', Myself would accept the Authority of the Believer-in 'I'. I mean The Believer-in 'I' don't have any authority, in true or spiritually over The Player-'I'."

"Submission physically means ?"

"A female Homo sapien being must not let its body to be viewed nakedly and touched by any organ of a male Homo sapien being other than Homo sapien being to whom it itself submitted. That male Homo sapien being to which it itself submitted can view its naked body when there is privacy for both. When there is privacy then only a female Homo sapien being has to let that male Homo sapien to touch itself."

"Shouldn't a male Homo sapien being touch a female Homo sapien being which accepted its authority where the public attention is snatched ?"

"Shouldn't. Touching each other of a male Homo sapien being and a female Homo sapien must be away from public attention."

"What will happen to a male Homo sapien being, if it views a naked female Homo sapien being ?"

"A lot of scope must be there for a male Homo sapien being to be affected vehemently."

"What about a female Homo sapien being who is naked and viewed by a male Homo sapien being other than the male Homo sapien being to whose authority it accepted ?"

"If a female Homo sapien being is done and done alike to such without her knowledge or intention, then, very little association would be adhered to her Mind for her headlessness or negligence or carelessness towards herself to be adorable. If done with intention or knowledge, her doing must be affected and fallen to be a Voluptuous being."

"Submission mentally means ?"

"No female Homo sapien being is ever allowed to lose its reason when it either notices or watches or looks or sees or views or observes or examines or minds or vigils or guards or surveillances a male Homo sapien being other than the male Homo sapien being whose authority it accepted."

"What will be so, if a female Homo sapien being is done ?"

"It would always be licentiousness."

"How can it be licentiousness ?"

"Licentiousness means sexually immoral. A female Homo sapien being is not at all a Voluptuous being to let any male Homo sapien being copulate it. You have already been told that a male Homo sapien being must stand for the Beingness which is the Chief character of The Only "I" who do 'Will' but not the doer of the deed. If a female Homo sapien being behaves as licentiousness, the Practice of the male Homo sapien being who is regarded as the Believer-in 'I' must be affected. Then both that male Homo sapien being and that female Homo sapien being must be affected and associations of them emanated accordingly would be adhered to. So, immortality is that which affects the Practice meant to regain the Unlost."

"Isn't a male Homo sapien being allowed to expect a female Homo sapien being of its choice to take part in copulation with itself ?"

"Never. A male Homo sapien being is never allowed to expect a female Homo sapien being of its choice even expect its own female Homo sapien being to which it married to take part in copulation whenever it gets desired. In reality, to 'desire' would be the first and foremost 'Doing' in the 'Many'. You are, I believe, perfectly extrapolated that 'Doing' would be of the female Homo sapien being i.e. the Player-'I' whose 'Doing' the Believer-in 'I' would grace."

"Do You mean the Believer-in 'I' must not 'do' anything ?"

"First of all You must bear in mind that 'gracing' is 'Doing' of the male Homo sapien being i.e. The Believer-in 'I'. Whatever, whichever, wherever and whenever the male

Homo sapien being i.e. The Believer-in 'I' would do must be in the Form of gracing only but not at all only in the form of either expecting some and enjoying that some or any."

"As a Homo sapien being, who too have organs of physical body, isn't it allowed to expect or enjoy ?"

"The Male Homo sapien being i.e. The Believer-in 'I' can expect an opportunity to grace not only The Female Homo sapien being i.e. the Player-'I' physically, mentally and spiritually but Another Male Homo sapien being i.e. another Believer-in 'I' spiritually only. The male Homo sapien being i.e. The Believer-in 'I' can enjoy whenever it can grace the Female Homo sapien being i.e. The Player-'I' who deserve to receive that 'gracing'."

"Can the Male Homo sapien being i.e. The Believer-in 'I' do grace the Female Homo sapien being i.e. The Player-'I' who don't deserve ?"

"When the Male Homo sapien being i.e. The Believer-in 'I' am not alert enough in observing The Practice meant to regain the Unlost, The Believer-in 'I' can grace The Player-'I'. But this gracing would be in the form of the favouring."

"Then what will happen ?"

"What else happen! The Practice of both The Believer-in 'I' and The Player-'I' would be certainly affected."

"When would The Believer-in 'I' be alert enough to grace the Player-'I' who deserve ?"

"When the Male Homo sapien being i.e. The Believer –in

'I' grace only one Female Homo sapien being i.e. only one Player-'I' by approving worshipping of The Player-'I' to be the better-half of The Believer-in 'I'."

"Approving the worshipping means ?"

"Approving the worshipping of The Player -'I' to be The better-half of The Believer-in 'I' whom The Player-'I' opt or select means the Marriage."

Chapter-37

"What is the Marriage ?"

"The Marriage is the Institution whereby the both Practitioners i.e. The Believer-in 'I' and The Player-'I' pinpoint the Ultimate End i.e. 'Regaining the Unlost' are joined to designate their own mission to be carried on by themselves and for themselves."

"Institution ! what sort of Institution is it ?"

"I narrate this Institution in the poetic manner. Listen to me carefully."

Tradition of wedding is for couples yet to be wedded.

'Rishies' bestow upon the Mankind this Institution that safeguards all.

'I', the Almighty endorse this establishment of envisioners.

No nation disapproves but suggests different forms and practices.

East is only enlightened early and the rest belatedly.

The tardy must obey the east obligatorily at each hour.

Humanity is, then, born to pervade everywhere on this earth.

Righteousness of Humanity is empowered to watch over humankind.

Each and every organism is for humankind and so is humankind.

Splendidness dances as its choice when righteous celebration is done.

Wooed woman worships wooer while viewing Him as Hers 'ever'.

After Future or beyond Future forever more flashes in this 'ever'.

Rules and regulations are framed for the comportment of both.

All enacted acts would be with reference to their deeds.

She is, therefore, honoured as 'SHE' who is without 'HE'.

History is intuited as "His"story" but which is of 'SHE'.

Albeit it is so, 'SHE' claims 'NOTHING' instead submits to 'Him'.

'SHE' could be 'HIS' better-half in all incarnations to be "S'HE'."

Tenets are manifested to preserve that which eternize the 'Being'.

Responsibility of either the observants or the Practitioners is kept on shoulders of wedded-couple.

Yeah, they are abided by, nonetheless, none could conceive in toto.

Sincere invitation is for all to rejuvenate of this institution.

Holy men favour this revitalization for this globe sanctified now as well.

Adult to infant enjoy and celebrate this auspicious ritual for all.

'I', the Almighty would graciously sacralize all uttered-blessings.

Love and Life of both would wrap each other of both.

All axioms get ratified and strengthened for the upcoming.

Juno and Jupiter walk through vestiges of "S'HE'" since now.

Ayes and awes are assuredly listened from all ten sides."

"Could I put some questions on this narrated poem ?"

"Yes. You can."

"What is Tradition ?"

"Handing down of opinions, beliefs, customs etc. from generation to generation is called as Tradition. The process of passing way of living from generation to generation is also called as Tradition. Any thing delivered from age to age is too called as Tradition."

"What is the generation and what is the age ?"

"The generation would mean single stage or step in family descent ; For instance grand parent is the first stage, parent is the second stage and child is the third stage of a family descent. If a thing i.e. a custom being practiced or observed from the first stage to the third stage would be the Tradition delivered from generation to generation."

"Age ?"

"The Age would mean the great or long period of the History of all living beings. But the History of all living beings would be recorded according to the Human History. Because the role of Human being is very particular, crucial, dominant, overbearing, overmastering, overriding, predominant, paramount and key for the entire organism. It has been almost concluded that History is of the Human beings only excluding all other beings. In this regard all other beings have been ignored and dishonoured. Whether Human being is representing all other beings or Human being has occupied the History isn't cleared."

"My question is of the Age ?"

"Before that You have to learn what is History actually. I tell it in poetic manner.

From fall of "I"
To reach of "I"
What I have done
Is only history
That is actually 'his'story
Which narrates

Only my story
When I have mistaken
My 'Self' for 'He'.

Here I stand for each and every 'I' who am "I" i.e. The Only "I". You have already been told that every each and every 'I' would have to regain the Unlost. To regain the Unlost is only the 'History' i.e. recorded or to be recorded of the Doing of the Practice each and every 'I'. This 'history' has been explained in this poem as 'his'story. Here 'his' means of each and every 'I'. So it could be well understood without having any doubt that each and every 'I' would stand for 'He' as every each and every 'I' would cherish the Illusion that every each and every 'I' am not The Only "I", so, every each and every 'I' would be regarded as 'He' i.e. third person instead of the first person i.e. The Only "I". Therefore it could be confirmed that History would be 'his'story i.e. the story of 'He' i.e. every each and every 'I' as 'He' would do the Practice meant to regain the Unlost. This 'doing' the Practice is only the story which would be the events of every each and every 'I' in the course of doing. It is to be noted that Mistaken My 'self' for 'He' would agree with cherishing the Illusion that every each and every 'I' am not The Only "I". But each and every 'I' who would enter into the body of Homo sapien being to indwell in, would be ignoring all other beings who would enter into the bodies of Voluptuous beings and totally forgetting that entering into the body of Homo sapien. It is a part and parcel of doing the Practice. This is the actual History which is being neglected.

"Now narrate what is the Age ?"

"You have already been told about the Time though it is True and Untrue and True and Untrue, it could be reckoned as it is existing and passing. This passing of Time could be divided into the Ages basing on the capability of Human beings, who are actually free from beastlihoodness to hold the righteousness. Thus the four Ages would come into existence respectively and repeat again and again respectively. During the First age, these Human beings who are free from beastlihoodness would behave with complete righteousness; During the second Age with three by four of righteousness; and During the third Age with two by four of righteousness and During the fourth Age with one by four of righteousness."

"When a Human being could not behave with complete righteousness during second, third and fourth Ages, how can that being accomplish its Practice perfectly ?"

"During those ages the Human being must go on keeping up to believe in The Only "I" while without detracting the attention towards The Only "I"."

"What is Wedding ? Is the Wedding a Tradition ?"

"Owing to the 'Will' done by The Only "I", You have been already told, all of each and every 'I' would cherish the Illusion that they would not be The Only "I" but each and every 'I'. Resulting in that cherishing, they would have to be in players of two roles. One of that group of players are the Players-'I' and another one the Believers-in 'I' for pinpointing the Ultimate End i.e. Regaining the Unlost. Then both would designate their own Mission to be carried on by themselves. This Designation is only the Marriage actually which had been got immediately when both The Player-'I' and The Believer-in 'I' would enter into the 'Many'. That Marriage is to be celebrated in each and every incarnation. This celebration is only the Wedding."

"How can all of us learn that particular couple had been same couple in the previous incarnation or incarnations, who used to get themselves wedded ?"

"A couple could get wedded in each and every incarnation. But it would depend upon the Player-'I'. When a player-'I' would spiritually worship a Believer-in 'I' in any incarnation, that player-'I' could get same Believer-in 'I' in forthcoming incarnations too."

"How ?"

"The casual body of any living being is not some other but it is the body free from all ingridients of 'the Many'. So this body is the spiritual body only. Though the casual body or the Spiritual body would be adhered to the association of every each and every 'I' and would be as each and every body to each and every 'I', the casual body or the Spiritual body would never be indivisible but it would be ever Only One who would be cherished as every each and every casual body to every each and every 'I'. In course of carrying on their own designated Mission, when a Player-'I' would spiritually worship herself opted or selected The Believer-in 'I', their Spiritual Union must be carried forward to the next incarnation. Accordingly The Player-'I' and The Believer-in 'I' would get wedded in the next incarnation at any cost let whatever hindrances play their roles. Hence, it is honoured as wedlock. If either this Player-'I' or this Believer-in 'I' fail to observe their this wed-lock as their own 'Marriage Vow'. None of both couldn't get married in current and forth coming some incarnation. So, failure one ought to resume the Practice to get married spiritually again. Now it is inevitable for counterpart to get another failure one to be its to partner to continue the Practice. So every wedded couple is obligatorily expected to observe their wedded-life as a 'Marriage Vow' in the current incarnation to continue as same couple in all forthcoming incarnations."

"Who are the 'Rishies' ?"

"Rishies are those who would envision what subject we have been having Talk."

"Is the Life, which would mould itself while getting wedded, the institution ? If so, how ?"

"Yes. The Life is the most important institution of the customs. The Life without being wedded is not at all the Life, it might be the breathing only. As far as concerned to Homo sapien beings, Life is the state of existence as human beings. When a Homo sapien being doesn't behave or act as a human being, that being can be taken granted for a being which is not in existence."

"Why are Homo sapien beings commanded alike ?"

"Because, Homo sapien beings are graced upon with 'Intellect'."

"Doesn't a female Homo sapien being or a male Homo sapien being have its own Life in separation ?"

"It could breath, behave, act and do as it is a separated

being from another being. But this 'it' or that 'it' doesn't have separate Life of its own."

"Why is it so ?"

"Not only Homo sapien being but Voluptuous being also doesn't have its own Life in separation in true. But Voluptuous being couldn't be aware of so even it couldn't learn the Life which is entwined with the lives of a male being and a female being."

"So, You have strong resolution that the Life is the Institution which deals with the wedded couple ?"

"Very properly You have stated."

"How could this Institution safeguard the mankind ?"

"When a male Homo sapien being and a female Homo sapien being would get wedded as per customs of clan and Lineage, then only, both as wedded couple enter into this Institution which would guide, check and control the couple, at first, not let the couple uncouples. Being a couple, no couple of Homo sapien being is, for good and all, expected to be uncoupled whichever cogent reason could be conspicuous there. The Player-'I' would instinctively worship The Believer-in 'I' and The Believer-in 'I' would spiritually grace The Player-'I'. Thus both The Player-'I' and The Believer-in 'I' would lead the Life while moulding that of each other. Therefore both could withstand what they are and wouldn't fall for the beastlihoodness."

"Why the East has been enlightened earlier to other sides ?"

"You know we are now having 'Talk' on the beings which would survive on the globe of the Earth only. From the Sun, which is honoured as the heavenly body, this Earth gets 'Warmth and light'. Warmth means the emotion. The emotion is a mental conscious reaction subjectively experienced as strong feeling usually directed toward a specific object and typically accompanied by physiological and behavioral changes in the body. Therefore, all the beings including human beings which are surviving in the East side of the Earth get warmth earlier to those which are surviving in the other sides of the Earth. Regarding to Emotion, the human beings could be more emotional and could express emotion and take in that emotion rather than all other beings. Hence the human beings i.e. Homo sapien beings could have the skill by dint of which they get experience or education. This skill is only the knowledge which is characterized as the Light. This knowledge is, thus, naturally gained by the human beings who are surviving in the East side of the Earth earlier to other human beings who are surviving in other sides of the Earth. Therefore, it is crystal clear that the human beings who are surviving in the East side of the Earth would be enlightened earlier to all other human beings who are surviving in other sides. Here, 'enlightenment' means giving more knowledge pertaining especially to The Only "I"."

"What is the Humanity ?"

"Humanity is a Virtue associated with basic ethics of Altruism derived from the human condition. Altruism is the principle and moral practice of concern for happiness of other human beings or animals, resulting in a quality of Life both material and spiritual. In an extreme case, Altruism may become a synonym of selflessness. The term Altruism may also refer to an ethical doctrine that claims that individuals are morally obliged to benefit others. So, it is usually contrasted with egoism. Hence, humanity must be pervaded everywhere on the Earth. Whereas all the Voluptuous beings would contain beastlihoodness, the Homo sapien beings i.e. the human beings must contain the Humanity and be free from the beastlihoodness."

"How can 'each and every organism' be for humankind and so be for humankind ?"

"Organism means an individual living being and humankind means all human beings as a group. Hence, organism could be applied for individual living human being too. Thus it can be accepted that humankind means all human beings along with all other beings than that of human as a group."

"How can it be accepted ?"

"In other way this item of subject has already been discussed. In the sense of the spirit, each and every being would be each and every 'I'. According to the Illusion cherished, some of each and every 'I' would indwell in the bodies Voluptuous beings and remaining of each and every 'I' would indwell in the bodies of Homo sapien beings. In course of and in the course of the Practice means to regaining the Unlost, each and every 'I' would enter into the body of Voluptuous body, leave that body, enter into the body of Homo sapien being, leave that body, enter into the body of same or another Voluptuous body leave that and enter into the body of another Homo sapien being. But it must be noted that no possibility would be there for every each and every 'I' to enter into and re-enter into same body of same Voluptuous being and go on entering into different sorts of bodies of different sorts of Voluptuous beings. It must also to be noted that no possibility would be there for every each and every 'I' to enter and re-enter same body of Homo sapien being. Thus it is to be learnt reincarnation would be there but no incarnation for same human being in any incarnation would be there. Thus it is crystal clear that each and every organism is for humankind and so is for humankind."

"Why should wooed woman worship wooer ?"

"At first woman must opt or select a man while viewing Him as Hers 'ever' means forevermore which would infer that for the endless Time. Here Time must be reckoned for The Present, The Future, beyond The Future and The Past which follow one after one respectively. When a woman i.e. The Player-'I' would opt or select thereby, then, The Believer-in 'I' would woo The Player-'I', The Player-'I' must not suppose to submit anything of hers to The Believer-in 'I'. The Believer-in 'I' would be allowed to woo only That Player-'I' who have opted or selected This Believer-in 'I'."

"Is the wooing not a doing ?"

"Very good question and very good clear question. Though The Believer-in 'I' would stand for the Beingness, The Believer-in 'I' would be too a doer. Because in The Believer-in 'I' there would be 'Doingness' too. It has already been discussed that in The Believer –in 'I', the Doingness would be less than that which is in the Player-'I'. It would have to be apparent to all of us that to a certain extent The Believer-in 'I' would be an only doer of 'wooing' The Player-'I' who would opt or select."

"Why would The Believer-in 'I' woo The Player-'I', when The Player-'I' opt or select The Believer-in 'I' ?"

"You must not either forget or overlook or ignore that The Player-'I' would be too The Only "I" whom The Believer-in 'I' believe-in. So The Believer-in 'I' would have to woo The Player-'I'. But The Believer-in 'I' must not woo any other Player-'I' who don't opt or select and worship this Believer-in 'I'. If The Believer-in 'I' don't woo that Player-'I' who have opted or selected and worshipped this Believer-in 'I', that Player-'I' couldn't worship another Believer-in 'I' notwithstanding The Player-'I' must not worship another Believer-in 'I'. The Player-'I' would at any time and at any cost be not permitted either to opt or select more than one Believer-in 'I' and worship. Even The Player –'I' would not be permitted to worship and submit to another Believer-in 'I' in the circumstances in which The Believer-in 'I', who is opted or selected or worshipped, don't woo that Player –'I'. Hence, The Believer-in 'I' must woo The Player-'I' who opt or select and worship this Believer-in 'I'. Even The Believer-in 'I' wouldn't be permitted to woo The Player-'I' as per choice of this Believer-in 'I'."

"If The Believer-in 'I' don't woo The Player-'I' who have opted or selected and worshipped this Believer-in 'I', then,..?

"Then, the associations emanated due to haven't wooed that Player-'I' would be adhered to this Believer-in 'I' and resulted in this Believer-in 'I' would be born as a Homo sapien being who couldn't have 'Self-respect' in any one of forthcoming incarnations."

"What about that Player-'I' ?"

"That Player-'I', though, would be born as The Player-'I' in all forthcoming incarnations, would go on as better-half of this Believer-in 'I' but spiritually that Player-'I' would be as The Player-'I' and would achieve the Ultimate End i.e. Regaining the Unlost."

"Despite this Believer-in 'I' would be born as The Believer-in 'I' who couldn't have 'Self-respect' in any one incarnations, would that Player-'I' worship this Believer-in 'I' ?'

"By all means."

"How ?"

"When The Player-'I' would worship The Believer-in 'I' whom The Player-'I' have opted or selected, the association emanated from worship would be adhered to that Player-'I'. The association, which has been emanated due to worshipping, would be of the spirit which would be Inseverable. So, that Player-'I' must go on to opt or select and worship this same Believer-in 'I' in forthcoming incarnations."

"In how many incarnations, that Player-'I' would opt or select and worship this Believer-in 'I' ?"

"Until this Believer-in 'I' learn the worshipping of that Player-'I' ?"

"Could that Player-'I' go on to opt or select and worship this Believer-in 'I' in each and every forthcoming incarnation ?"

"Can't be ?"

"How ?"

"In an instant of second, a lot of scope would be there for that Player-'I' to breach the self restricted principles and clauses for worshipping The Believer-in 'I', within no second that Player-'I' would cherish the Illusion that Player-'I' would not be for this Believer-in 'I' or this Believer-in 'I' would not be The Believer-in 'I' whom that Player-'I' have not opted or selected and worshipped. So, can't be."

"Then, what will happen ?"

"When that Player-'I' would cherish, in any incarnation, the Illusion that Player-'I' would not be for this Believer-in 'I' or this Believer-in 'I' would not be The Believer-in 'I' whom that Player-'I' have not opted or selected and worshipped, then, that Player-'I' would be no other but the Voluptuous being. Therefore, this fallen each and every 'I' who have fallen from the Player-'I' to the Voluptuous being in an incarnation would have to re-achieve the state to be the Player-'I' while indwelling in the body of Homo sapien being in any forthcoming incarnations and commence the Practice to regain this Believer-in 'I' in course of doing the Practice to regain the Unlost."

"Could You expound who is 'SHE' ?"

"I expound 'SHE' in a poetic manner. Listen !

Whatever She experiences,
Whichever She obtains
Whenever She conjuctures
All He would receive
As she ever contains He

Who am actually 'I'
Who is ever mistaken for 'I'
But himself mistakes for 'He'.

Two items of the Subject are to be noted here. He would be He who am The Only "I" whom SHE contains in, so, SHE would be too The Only "I'. Therefore, SHE would be Two in One."

"SHE would be Two in One ?"

"Yes. You must keep on Your Mind that The Player-'I' would be for Doing and The Believer-in 'I' for Being. It must as well be kept on Your Mind that though The Believer-in 'I' would be for Being, The Believer-in 'I' would also be for Doing in this regard i.e. the communion between The Player-'I' and The Believer-in 'I' meant to be One physically, mentally and spiritually. Therefore both The Player-'I' and The Believer-in 'I' would be the Doers. Except wooing The Player-'I', The Believer-in 'I' would not attend any other doing pertaining to the Practice meant to regain the Unlost. The Player-'I' only would attend every other doings pertaining to the Practice meant to regain the Unlost. Hence, there would be Two to do practice meant to regain the Unlost. As long as these Two would be separate from each other in the Practice to regain the Unlost, both would be One and One only. When The Player-'I' would opt or select and worship The Believer-in 'I' who would grace that Player-'I', then, That Player-'I' would be Two in one."

"How could this 'Two in One' be to have been viewed ?"

"This 'Two in One' could be as 'Two is only One' Listen to me, I narrate this 'Two is only One' in poetic manner.

Not You are away from 'I',
Not beyond 'I' and beside 'I',

In dream and in imagination;
In thought and in mind;

In words and in lyrics;
In doings and in deeds;

In looks and in signs;
In laughs and in sighs;

In tastes and in aesthetics;
In silence and in meditation;

In waiting and in receiving;
In heart and in breath.

As two, one had made every effort
With best to be Two in each other.

But 'Two' has been ever succeeding
To withstand as One to be only 'One'.

Therefore the couple who gets wedded must be graced as 'SHE' when they would be for each other."

"What would be the Dissimilitude between 'SHE' and "S'HE'" ?"

"In the poem You have just listened, You can easily have comprehended that though both The Player-'I' and The Believer-in 'I' would have succeeded to be only 'One', they would have still their own conscious in separation regarding from dream to breath. This 'Conscious' has continued upto the point or the point of Time to be cherished as Time. Two i.e. both The Player-'I' and The Believer-in 'I' have been succeeding to withstand as 'One'. When this succeeding could get The Player-'I' and The Believer-in 'I' to withstand as 'One' forever, since then, The Player-'I' and The Believer-in 'I' would be 'SHE'. This 'SHE', since now, would maintain to be as SHE until this 'SHE' would accomplish to be as "S'HE'". This "S'HE'" could be physically as The Player-'I' or as The Believer-in 'I' but none could learn with certainty whether this "S'HE'" would be The Player-'I' or The Believer-in 'I'. Because it is unthinkable to all others to ascertain whether 'She' i.e. The Player-'I' have achieved to be "S'HE'" in whom 'He' as 'HE' or The Believer –in 'I' have achieved to be "S'HE'" in whom 'He' has been come out as 'HE' who would be The Only "I". That is the Dissimilitude between 'SHE' and "S'HE'"."

Chapter-38

"When The Player-'I' would worship The Believer-in 'I' and The Believer-in 'I' woo that Player-'I' and both This Believer-in 'I' and That Player-'I' would be all right visualized as they have been already married spiritually in the beginning of the 'Many' come into existence by the 'Will' done by The Only "I", then, is the celebration of Wedding indispensable ?"

"Yes. it is indispensable."

"Why ?"

"Because, though the Marriage would have been got spiritually in the beginning of the 'Many', it could not be visioned physically and envisioned mentally. Therefore celebration of Wedding of The Player-'I' to The Believer-in 'I' must be done whenever That Player-'I' worship This Believer-in 'I' who grace That Player-'I' ."

"Upto the extent of Wedding, it must be done. But why should that Wedding be celebrated ?"

"For Social Acceptance."

"Why is the Social Acceptance warranted ?"

"I narrate it in Poetic manner. Listen!

> Wedding is auspiciously being celebrated.
> Invitees from both sides are attending.
> Among them, Kith and Kin and others are too.

From kids to grown up could be found there.
But both kids and grown up would be same.
Jest, joke, comic, pun etc. are the Humour only.

Age, dignity, decency and protocol are ignored.
All of them sing and play but none is defeated.
No rewards but Awards are conferred on all.

Dinner is special but none is special at dinner.
Differed tongues taste same taste at dinner.
All bless pair to accept but not to be witness."

"Can I put some questions ?"

"Yes. You can."

"Why is Wedding celebrated auspiciously ?"

" 'Auspicious' means showing signs, giving promise of future success; also fortunate. All those, who would organize and participate in this celebration and attend it, must have to show their signs which indicate that the couple, which is getting wedded, can lead life during which they never be uncoupled whichever circumstances aroused that may cause to misunderstand each other. While expressing well-wishings, all the concerned to that ceremony would give promise indirectly or directly to the couple which would succeed in its wedded-life. So, that couple must be fortunate in their Mission. For the couple to be fortunate, 'Wedding' must be celebrated auspiciously."

"How could 'signs, promises and wishes' be so effected ?"

"You have to recollect the Poem told to Your question on

Marriage and its Poetic line,

'I', the Almighty would graciously sacralize all uttered-blessings'."

"Yes, I have to do so.Would 'I', The Almighty, Who am beyond all beings and all things, sacralize?"

"By all means. No doubt 'I', the Almighty i.e. The Only "I" would be beyond all beings and all things. Among all beings, those, who would have expressed 'signs, promises and wishes,' would be there. You know, I am sure, these would only be The Only "I". when these would express so without any intention to be quenched in 'the Many', then, that 'expressions' must be of The Spirit i.e. of The Only "I". Hence all uttered-blessings must be sacralized irrefutably, incontrovertibly and indubitably."

"Why should invitees be from both sides ?"

"Though the invitees would be from various lineages, they must be germane to the same society which is comprised of the Lineages from the same 'clan' or 'caste'. All those, who are from the same society, are akin to one another. As long as each and every 'I' would be under inexplicable impact of The Illusion, that each and every 'I' would have 'attachment' that either The Player-'I' who am going to get wedded or The Believer-in 'I' who am going to wed The Player-'I' would be 'mine' i.e. of that each and every 'I'. So, each and every 'I' instinctively wish that either The Player-'I' whom each and every 'I' would take as 'mine' or The Believer-in 'I' whom each and every 'I' would do as 'mine' must be graced upon 'the Achievement' of the Mission of the Marriage. So, among invitees those, from both sides, should be there."

"Would we, each and every 'I', be aware of our Achievement and Mission ?"

"Physically and Mentally we can not be but Spiritually we would be. Owing not to be aware of so physically and mentally, most of us are unable either to make out or perceive or grasp or apprehend or extrapolate or comprehend the Marriage and its celebration as Wedding."

"Why are most of us unaware of ?"

"Owing to be under impact of Illusion."

"Why should Kith and Kin and others be there ?"

"First of all You should keep on Your mind that all invitees from both sides, Kith and Kin and others are those who are every each and every 'I' who am actually The Only "I". Kith are friends and Kin are relatives. A Friend of a Homo sapien being is too a Homo sapien being whom earlier Homo sapien being knows and likes well. Except Homo sapien being, possibility wouldn't be there for any Voluptuous beings to have a friend from same sort of Voluptuous beings. But it is strange to believe that a Voluptuous being from any sort can be a friend to a Homo sapien being. Hence, it would be understood that friendship would be possible between or among Homo sapien being only. So, a Voluptuous being, which can be as a friend to a Homo sapien being, would have innerly and inconspicuously sturdy part of character of Homo sapien being. Lot of scope for the eventuality would be there for few Voluptuous beings from various sorts to attend that celebration of Wedding though they are not naturally invited. Hence, it is clear that The Friendship is too a 'Tie' like wed-lock. This 'Tie' would be in effect from incarnation to incarnation and in some cases through out incarnations. Hence forward a Relative of a Homo sapien being is a member of family of that Homo sapien being or a Homo sapien being connected with another Homo sapien being by blood or affinity. So, it is cleared that relatives are those who are members of the family. Hence great grand parents to great grandsons and great grand daughters are relatives to one another. Without their knowledge, they approve or endorse that celebration and let the couple observe its practice and act as friends of it and help it to cause its practice not to be prevented or obstructed in any manner. It is also cleared that there is another relative who is connected by blood or affinity. A relative connected by blood can be from same family or another family from Lineage. This relative can too act as a relative who is among great grand parent to great grand child. The relative, who is connected by affinity, is not a relative among great grand parent to great grand child or from a family or a Lineage. This relative connected by affinity would be so who must be invited, honoured, regarded, respected even venerated without ignoring under any circumstances. Because relation with this relative is connected by the Affinity which is the feeling of the inward and understanding brought forth from similar qualities, ideas or interests. Owing to have this affinity, all those relatives come together mentally. The mental relationship would cause all those each and every 'I' who have affinity towards one another to make for the Spiritual relationship. Therefore Kith and Kin who would cordially, sincerely, whole heartedly, genuinely, fervently and blithesomely bless the couple going to be wedded in the light of the Practice meant to regain the Unlost."

"Actually what is Affinity ?"

"You have already just been told that the Affinity is the conscious feeling which would be just differed from all other feelings. I will try to narrate it in Poetic manner. Listen to me carefully.

The indivisible, "I", though, 'i' look as 'i' and 'i'
Behaved as only 'i' but not as 'i' and 'i' ever.

Until 'i' and 'i' have known and learnt 'i' and 'i'
Actually would be only 'i' but not 'i' and 'i' ever.,

'i' and 'i' have not to do will to beget 'i' of 'i'
From 'i' to do what 'i' do to be 'i' like 'i' and 'i'.

'i' and 'i' have decisively known and learnt that
'i' and 'i' was Only "I" and ought to be 'i' at first.

To be Only "I" while acting as 'i' and 'i', 'i' do to
Beget 'i' and bring up 'i' to be 'i' to bring 'i' out.

Both brought up and out 'i' and 'i' from different
Parents must be made to learn 'i' and 'i' am "I".

So, begotten 'i' have been born as 'i' and have
Been envisaging another 'i' who am same 'i'.

Though, the term begotten clearly bespeaks
'i' and 'i' are there and from separate parents.

But parents are too 'i' and 'i' who did as only 'i',
Dissimilar parents have also followed earlier.

As the earlier Learned, the Parents could know
And learn to which 'i' could follow which 'i' ever."

"Who are others ?"

"Whoeverelse. Others are those who can be like Kith and Kin in the letter of idea and spirit."

"Should those, who aren't among Kith and Kin and others, not be invited ?"

"Should not be. If it is done, the Decisiveness of the celebration can be affected."

"Are Jest and Joke, Comic and Pun etc. Which are Humour necessary in that celebration ? If so what are they ? What is the Humour ?"

"Yes. All they are necessary. Jest is an utterance intended to be taken for a frivolous mood. So It can be done by all from kid to grown up as no decency can be damaged. Joke is something said or done to cause amusement i.e. entertainment. Entertainment is to show hospitality which means generous and friendly treatment of guests. So, where celebration of Wedding is done, all invitees must be treated friendly. Friendly treatment is that which pleases all equally and uniformly and doesn't degrade or disparage any in any manner. In this celebration, The Player-'I' and The Believer-in 'I', who are in true The Only "I", would get wedded. Like The Player-'I' and The Believer-in 'I' all the organizers and the invitees are too The Only "I". When The Player-'I' and The Believer-in 'I', by dint of Wedding, are going to fortify and strengthen their Practice meant to regain the Unlost, all, who would be in that celebration, would have to bless that celebration in course of observing their Practice. It is the Blessing which must be done beyond all feelings and emotions pertaining to 'the Many'. When the invitees would bless accordingly, during uttering of words of blessing, they could be like The Only "I". Thus they would be fortified and strengthened. In addition, All participants including organizers and invitees must initiate to bring forth the comic moment in the course of Wedding-celebration. The comic moment is, generally and normally, accepted that during which all who are on the spot, could enjoy the comedy which is impeccable. So, during that moment all organizers and invitees would be impeccable, so, all they would go on in that moment as The Only "I" in this 'Many'. It is to be noted that The Only "I" would forever more be impeccable. The Pun means humourous use of words which sound the same or two meanings of the same word. So, it is clear that A pun is like a Joke that makes a play on words. Before the Past, there had been only one word i.e. "I". You have already been told that even the words 'Be' and 'Do' had not been there. When that "I", who had been only before the Past, have done 'Will' to be 'Many', since then only, more than one words have come into existence. All those words are The Only "I" but are cherished as 'Many'. Like that when a word sounds more meanings than one, that would only be The Only "I". So, Pun must be exercised in this celebration. Now, the Humour ! All Jest, Joke, Comic and Pun etc. are the Humour or of the Humour. Actually Humour means capacity to cause or feel the Amusement. So, there are two things to be noted that one is to cause and another one is to feel. Hence it must sagaciously be learnt that The Only "I" would cause 'the Many' while doing the 'Will' and each and every 'I', who have cherished that each and every 'I' am not The Only "I", would be conscious of an inward impression that each and every 'I' would do the Practice meant to regain the Unlost. So, as a Homo sapien being, each and every human being must have sense of humour. Because, Humour doesn't mean the Amusement straightly. It is the capacity to cause or feel.

The Only "I" would be capable from the beginninglessness to the endlessness to be in the form of the Bliss in which form neither complications nor difficulties nor hardships nor miseries nor vexes nor afflictions nor distresses nor tribulations etc. couldn't be found. The Only "I" would be Omni-potent, so, The Only "I" would be in the form of the Bliss. During 'the Many', whenever the Amusement is arisen, during that period too complications to tribulations can not be found. Hence, the Humour is invited in this celebration which is the chief auspicious deed of the Practice meant to regain the Unlost."

"Why are the Age, the Dignity, the Decency and the Protocol ignored ?"

"I have told You that at the celebration of the Wedding from the organizers to the invitees all are The Only "I". Because, only those Player-'I' and Believer-in 'I' who have been spiritually married in the beginning of 'the Many' are only got Wedded in 'the Many'. During the celebration of Wedding, every each and every 'I' of all the invitees and the organizers would bless that couple. Hence it is clear that The Player-'I' and The Believer-in 'I' and every each and every 'I' of all organizers and invitees would be The Only "I" who have not been born and who never die. Thus, to calculate the Age of all could not be possible. Actually there would be no age for every each and every 'I' of all the organizers and the invitees along with The Player-'I' and The Believer-in 'I'. Hence, nobody would be elder or Younger. Thereby the Dignity would be enjoyed by each and every 'I'. Actually wedding is only the celebration of the Marriage which had already got spiritually. All those, who would be either organizers or invitees in this celebrations, have been spiritually married, though, the Wedding-celebration might be done or not. Therefore, each and every one at Wedding-celebration would deserve respect to be paid. Hence, the Dignity must be ignored. Next the Decency; for the Decency only Kith and Kin and the others, who can be like Kith and Kin in the letter of idea and spirit, can only be invited. All these Kith and Kin and these others would observe the Decency i.e. to be modest. Hence, all in that wedding-celebration behave decently so that attention is not required to pay on all among whom any one or few might not behave decently resulting in the wedding-celebration can be affected. Eventually the Protocol; Only the celebration of wedding of a couple i.e. The Player-'I' and The Believer-in 'I' can be done earlier to another couple i.e. another The Player-'I' and The Believer-in 'I'. But the 'Marriage' of earlier and later couple has been got simultaneously. Hence, Regarding to the Wedding-celebration of Marriage only, a couple can be earlier and another couple later. But regarding to the 'Marriage' none would be earlier or later. Hence, no protocol must be observed."

"How can none be defeated in singing and playing ?"

"Regarding to singing, I narrate in poetic manner. Listen !

While I sing
I never find
As somebody listens to.

While I accompany
With something or without anything
I never find
As mine flashes even for little long.

In that singing
While I listen to

I never find
Any kind of distinction
Between or among
Singing, accompanying and listening.

While I am in 'Singing'
I never get consciousness of
What is beyond 'Singing'
Even for any little duration.

While 'Singing' continues
I never find
Even my'self' as I am.

Till 'Singing' lasts
No participant could suppose
Even for the least span of time
As he is in 'Singing'.

Hence, it could be understood that all the participants i.e. the Singer, the Accompanist and the Listeners in the singing would not get any consciousness of what is beyond 'Singing'. Even none of the Singer, the Accompanist and the Listener oneself as either the Singer or the Accompanist or the Listener is beyond the 'singing ? Thus all would be there as Only 'One'. When there is 'One' qualified by adjective 'Only', that 'One' would be never another but The Only "I". Because, all the Singer, the Accompanist and the Listener would not be 'Many', which has been come into existence by the 'Will' done by The Only "I". Who would be 'One' from beginningless to endlessness, but 'One' only i.e. The Only "I". During the Wedding-celebration, all the 'Singing' would pertain to communion of The Player-'I' and The Believer-in 'I'. Hence, no question of the defeat could be arisen. Regarding to the Playing it is to be noted that as a noun, 'Play' means 'Drama' for the stage and as a verb, 'Play' means 'Perform' a drama on the stage. Regarding to the meaning of 'Drama', I narrate in poetic manner. Listen to me.

Is it Truth ?
Not at all it is.

Is it Untruth ?
At any cost it isn't.

Isn't it Truth ?
No doubt it is.

Isn't it Untruth ?
Very certainly it is.

Actually what it is ?
It am only "I".

Who am "I" ?
"I" am undefinable.

Why am "I" alike ?
So only "I" am.

How am "I" Truth ?
"I" exist as invisible.

How am "I" Untruth ?
"I" am understood as visible.

Why do "I" do as so ?
"I" am everything and everyone.

Why am "I" done as so ?
"I" am for spectators.

Hence, it must be conceived that the Drama is not Truth nor Untruth but the Drama is Truth and Untruth as well. Because, like The Only "I", the Drama would be too undefinable. During 'the Many' does exist, The Only "I" couldn't be visible to all those who are each and every 'I'. In the course of the Practice to regain the Unlost, The Only "I" would be gradually understood even envisioned at last as each and every 'I' am The Only "I". Here it is to be noticed that observing or doing the Practice would be the Playing of the Drama which would be no other thing but 'the Many' only. When observing or doing the Practice described as the Playing of the Drama, then, every each and every 'I' would be Players of 'the Many' i.e. the Drama. In this Drama, 'the Many', which doesn't end upto the 'Will' for 'Not to be Many' done by The Only "I", no 'Defeat' for any Player i.e. each and every 'I' as all the Players i.e. every each and every 'I' would go on observing or doing the Practice from the 'Many' to the 'Many' while being kept under the rest during the periods of the 'Not to be Many' to the 'Not to be Many' until each and every 'I' i.e. Player of Drama of 'the Many' achieve the End i.e. Regaining the Unlost."

"Why won't be rewards but only awards ?"

"Because, only The spirit of all who organize and who are invited would bless The Married-Spirit of The Player-'I' and The Believer-in 'I'. The spirit would be that which would be beyond the Matter which affects the Mind and the Body of The Player-'I' and The Believer-in 'I'. Hence, there wouldn't be question of affecting the Married spirit. So, no rewards would be conferred on both. Owing to the blessings of the spirit of all the organizers and the invitees, the spirit of The Player-'I' and The Believer-in 'I' would be espoused literally. Therefore, the Awards which strengthen the Practice of both must be conferred on them."

"In which form the Awards be conferred on ?"

"In the next incarnation these Homo sapien beings i.e. The Player-'I' and The Believer-in 'I', whose Marriage got wedded in the form of celebration and the spirit of them received the Blessings from the spirit of all the organizers and the invitees would take birth with less Voluptuousness than that of the Present incarnation in the forthcoming incarnation. Taking birth with less Voluptuousness would be the Award."

"Why should the Dinner be special ?"

"The Dinner is an impressive meal for many people usually to celebrate special event. The celebration of Wedding would be generally a planned occasion intended to until The Player-'I' with The Believer-in 'I' to observe their Practice jointly to regain the Unlost. Thus, the Wedding-ceremony would be of the World i.e. the Matter and the spirit of both which would be beyond the World i.e. the Matter. Therefore, this ceremony could be honoured and venerated as the Most Auspicious Deed and must be done. Keeping in view of Auspiciousness of Marriage got spiritually and the Wedding to be celebrated during 'the Many', The Dinner must be arranged accordingly. In this Dinner very delicious items of food must be served. But the Dinner must be the cuisine based on local ingridients. The cuisine based on non-local ingredients might affect the constitution of all who are in that wedding. It must be seen that though there is the local cuisine, all the items must be delicious which delight all. In this celebration, the Delightedness only must be disseminated to all over the Premises where the celebration being conducted. For this delightedness of each and every one, the Dinner shall be served but keeping in view one or few not be done as Wedding-celebration must be done to the spirit but not to the sense-pleasure."

"Are all the invitees to bless only but not to be witness ?"

"Yes. all the invitees are prayed to bless only. They are not at all to be witness of the Wedding. Because the wedding would not be at all an agreement to be executed; nor an accord something as special treatment; nor a concurrence of agreeing with someone; nor a concord with each other; nor a contract to be executed between each other; nor a live-in with someone. When The Player-'I' and The Believer-in 'I' enter into 'the Many' at that point of Time only both would enter as the spiritually Married-couple. Owing to their cherishing Illusion that they would not be The Only "I", so, they have entered into 'the Many' as the Player 'I' who would indwell in the body of female-sex and The Believer –in 'I' who would indwell in the body of male sex. In the perceptible 'Many', the wedding would be taken granted for as a wedding of a female Homo sapien being and a male Homo sapien being. But the Marriage should only be celebrated as the Wedding which wouldn't be an agreement, an accord, a concurrence, a concord, a contract and a live-in to be witnessed. The Only "I" would forever be the spectator of all deeds being done in course of the entire Practice observed to regain the Unlost. Hence, among every each and every 'I', who would organize or be invited, could not witness. Further, it is to be noted that every each and every 'I' i.e. the organizers, the Invitees and the couple which would go to wed are The Only "I", so, every each and every 'I' am myself the Spectator for each and every doing of every each and every 'I'."

Chapter-39

"What would be wrong with The Believer-in 'I', if The Believer-in 'I' woo a player-'I' who don't worship This Believer-in 'I' ?"

"If it so happened, two things would happen. First, The Believer –in 'I' must be degraded in the view of The Player-'I' and The Player-'I', if, am allured, The Player-'I' wouldn't worship This Believer-in 'I' or any other Believer-in 'I' but The Player-'I' can behave with This Believer-in 'I' as a Voluptuous being. Resulting in, no Love Making could be possible when they participate in copulation."

"What is Love Making ?"

"At present stage, You can't imagine it."

"When do I can ?"

"It too can't be imagined."

"How can I understand it ?"

"When You and I could behave as The Player-'I' who do worship The Believer-in 'I' and The Believer-in 'I' do woo The Player-'I' who do worship this The Believer-in 'I', then only, You and I can experience it but couldn't express out that experience."

"For both The Player –'I' and The believer –in 'I', to experience the Love Making is must ?"

"Yes."

"Then, what should the wedded The Player-'I' who have worshipped The Believer-in 'I' and The Believer-in 'I' who have graced The Player do to get experience of Love Making ?"

"In the course of worshipping The Believer-in 'I' at each and every second, The Player-'I' would gradually ignore Her'Self'. Ignoring One 'Self' is only the Ultimate stage of the worship."

"Is or are any prescribed methods there to worship ?"

"No such methods are there. If any such method is told, it couldn't be perfect at all. Because, to worship someone would be choice of worshipper. To worship means to regard with respect, honour and devotion."

"What would be wrong with The Player-'I', if The Player-'I' adopt a method prescribed by someone ?"

"The Player-'I' wouldn't succeed in that worship."

"Why ?"

"Every each and every 'I', who have entered in this 'Many' as The Player –'I', have entered with her own level or range of 'Doingness'. According to that level or range, every each and every Player-'I' have initiated the Doing of the Deeds of every each and every Player-'I' not in common or in the same way or manner but the way or manner of every each and every initiation has been quite different from one another."

"Then ?"

"Then, each and every 'I' must adopt peculiar method which

could not be compared or likened."

"How can every each and every Player-'I' learn separate or own initiation of every each and every Player-'I' that couldn't be compared or likened with one another ?"

"When the Marriage of The Player-'I' has been got to The Believer-in 'I' in the earliest beginning of existence of 'the Many' come due to the 'Will' done by The Only "I", spiritually The Player-'I' could learn The Believer-in 'I' to whom The Player-'I' should worship and how to do so. But The Player-'I' could not express that worship physically or mentally. In spite of That Player-'I' would be unable to express, That Player-'I' instinctively initiate the worshipping of The Believer-in 'I' to whom That Player-'I' have been got married. So, the worshipping would be done instinctively. Therefore, every each and every Player-'I' would have separate inborn or innate or inherent or inbred character of worshipping The Believer –in 'I' who have married."

"Could every each and every Player-'I' learn so and worship only The Believer-in 'I' who have married ?"

"For every each and every Player-'I' it could not be possible."

"Why ?"

"When The Player-'I' could enter into the body of Homo sapien being without any emanated associations that would cause any quantity of Voluptuousness in body of Homo sapien being into which That Player-'I' to have entered, it could be possible to That Player-'I' to learn which Believer-in 'I' am to be worshipped."

"Can't The Player-'I', who have entered into the body of Homo sapien being with some emanated associations from previous incarnation or incarnations that cause some quantity or quantity of Voluptuousness in that body of Homo sapien being, be able to pinpoint or distinguish spiritually The Believer-in 'I' who have married spiritually ?"

"Can't be possible."

"How can The Player-'I', who am in such state in which That Player can't be able to pinpoint or distinguish spiritually The Believer-in 'I' who have married spiritually, be able to do so ?"

"Very crucial question it is which You put. For every each and every Player-'I' who have entered into the body of Homo sapien beings with Voluptuousness due to the associations emanated in the Previous incarnation or incarnations, it is hardly possible to learn the distinction between wish and desire, love and like and worship and crazy. So, every each and every Player-'I' must make every effort with best to check and control desire, like and crazy. Owing to be indwelling in the body of Homo sapien being, That Player-'I' would have an advantage to select one of every each and every Believer-in 'I' who am too indwelling in the body of Homo sapien being with some quantity of Voluptuousness. As a Player-'I', The Player-'I' would be, however, a Doer. So, The Player-'I' could wish The selected Believer-in 'I' to be of her. As long as The Player-'I' can keep her 'wishing' as wishing only without letting that wishing descend upto desiring, The Player-'I' can be a Player-'I' who have not fallen from the current state and That Player-'I' would be adhered to association of worshippingness emanated. Therefore, That Player-'I' can be able to distinguish or pinpoint spiritually The Believer-in 'I' who have married That Player-'I' spiritually. Until then, That

Player-'I' should go on selecting The Believer-in 'I' to wish. If this selected Believer-in 'I' don't either receive the wish of that Player-'I' or respond to this wish favourably, that Player-'I' must not change attitude and select another Believer-in 'I' in lieu of That Believer-in 'I'. This is the celebacy of That Player-'I' to be maintained in the current incarnation while fancying This Believer-in 'I' as The Believer-in 'I' who have married spiritually. If The Player-'I' do so, then, That Player-'I' can be able to worship The Believer-in 'I' who have actually married spiritually."

"Can The Player-'I', who behaves like You have just told, be able to worship That Believer-in 'I' who have actually married spiritually."

"Very rarely it can be possible. But it must be possible in any one of forthcoming incarnations."

"When it can be possible very rarely ?"

"When The Player-'I' select The Believer-in 'I', who have actually married spiritually, in the current incarnation without having the knowledge of distinction in selecting due to have been with Voluptuousness, it can be possible. It may be very rarely but it couldn't be a strange. It is very rare because The Player-'I' couldn't distinguish to worship but without having spiritual attachment which couldn't be known, learnt and understood to both That Player-'I' and This Believer-in 'I'."

"What will happen, if The Player-'I' does desire The Believer-in 'I' who have been selected by The Player-'I' ?"

"That Player-'I' must be adhered to some more association

or associations of Voluptuousness emanated by desiring. Resulting in that Player-'I' would be more Voluptuous in forthcoming incarnation or incarńations, though, that Player-'I' would indwell in the body of Homo sapien being. Then also same situation would be there."

"Then, what about The Believer-in 'I' ?"

"The Believer-in 'I' would be so who would ever maintain celibacy in The Only "I" who am no other but This Believer-in 'I' only. So, This Believer-in 'I' must keep the 'Beingness' of The Believer-in 'I' who must grace the worshipping of The Player-'I' only. This Believer-in 'I' must not be pleased with any doing of The Player-'I' other than doing of worshipping; When The Believer-in 'I' descend from the gracing That Player-'I' to being got pleases with any other doing of The Player-'I', This Believer-in 'I' also must be adhered to the more association or the associations of Voluptuousnes emanated."

"What will happen, if both The Player-'I' and The Believer-in 'I' would be adhered to the association or associations accordingly ?"

"The Practice meant to regain the Unlost would be affected in the worst way."

"How will be that ?"

"Regaining the Unlost would be delayed. Even it couldn't be possible in the duration of last second of 'the Many' after elapsing which The Only "I" do 'Will' 'Not to be Many' which would last as long as 'the Many' lasts. It couldn't be also possible in the next 'Many' which would follow 'Not to be

Many'. It is further not assumed that in which 'Many' it could be possible. Hence, the Practice would have to be observed from 'the Many' to 'the Many' would have to be observed from 'the Many' to 'the Many' while going on as incapable to do anything in each and every 'Not to be Many' which would either follow or precede each and every 'the Many'."

"Can the Possibility be there either for The Player-'I' to distinguish or pinpoint The Believer-in 'I' whom The Player-'I' would have to actually select or opt or for The Believer-in 'I' to grace The Player-'I' who actually worship This Believer-in 'I' ?"

"Assuredly."

"How ?"

"When The Player-'I' am imparted with traditions and customs of Lineage and clan, then, The Player-'I' could be checked and controlled by Her'Self'. This checked and controlled Player-'I' could be only educated with the subject of the spirit. The Learned in the subject of the spirit from the same Lineage or the same clan or from other Lineage or other clan would educate That Player-'I' while either teaching or preaching. If The Player-'I' observe all traditions and customs of the Lineage or the clan in which The Player-'I' am born, That Player-'I' My'Self' gain or acquire the knowledge of the spirit. Though The Player-'I' gain or acquire the knowledge of the spirit, The Player-'I' couldn't express it out. Even those Learned who have educated The Player-'I' also couldn't express it out."

"Can 'I' put two questions on which You have just told ?"

"Yes. You can."

"My first question :- Can the Learned, who are from other Lineage or clan, educate The Player-'I' to gain the knowledge of the spirit ? If so, could those Learned have gained the knowledge of the spirit of the Lineage or the Clan of That Player-'I' ?"

"All the Learned from same Lineage or Clan of That Player-'I' would be the Learned of the knowledge of the spirit. 'The Spirit', which would be known and learnt, would be only 'One' for all Lineages and clans. Besides, any Learned of the knowledge of the spirit would only educate The Player-'I' or The Believer-in 'I'' but no Learned from any Lineage or clan could preach or teach the knowledge of the Spirit. To educate The Player-'I' means the Learned from any Lineage or clan could develop The Player-'I' mentally, morally and aesthetically especially by institution. On being developed accordingly, The Player-'I' My 'Self' must gain the knowledge of the Spirit."

"My second question :- Why can't those Learned from any Lineage or Clan who have educated The Player-'I' also express the knowledge of the spirit out ?"

"Actually The Only "I" would be the spirit which would consistently be beyond 'the Many' in which every each and every 'I' would be. Being beyond means none or nothing could affect or influence the Spirit. Every each and every 'I' would be the indivisible Spirit in Nature and Character. When The Player-'I' or The Believer-in 'I' conceive the Nature of the Spirit, it would be knowledge of That Player-'I' or This Believer-in 'I'; when The Player-'I' or The Believer –in 'I' conceive the character of the Spirit, it would be the Learning of That Player –'I' or This Believer-in 'I'. Nature of the Spirit means basic construction of the Spirit. The construction of the spirit would be of the Spirit only. Except spirit, no any other perceptible or imperceptible thing would be there in the construction of the Spirit. The character of the Spirit would be the consciousness from which the Spirit could do even which couldn't be ever imagined. Though the Spirit could have done any, the Spirit could never be attached with what the spirit would do. Thus, the Learned could conceive the spirit but couldn't explain the spirit which would beyond all among in which the Language would be also there."

"Having been controlled or checked by Her'Self' would mean what ?"

"You have to learn the word, Her'Self'. Actually the Self would be nothing but the Spirit which would be indivisible. All the 'selves' i.e. Her'Self', My'Self', Your'Self' and It'Self' would be only the 'Self' in true. I mean for the 'Self', there would not be plurality. But when an each and every 'I' take myself would be separate from Yourself under the impact of the Illusion, then only, the 'Selves' i.e. the plurality might flash for a while which is the duration of 'the Many'. Hence, conceiving the spirit means envisioning of all 'Selves' as the Self. As long as The Player-'I' or The Believer-in 'I' or The Learned are in 'the Many', either The Player-'I' or The Believer-in 'I' or The Learned would be one of selves only but could not be the Self. When Having been controlled or checked by Her'Self'. When Having been controlled or checked by Her 'Self' not Her'Self' or the 'Self', then, That Player-'I' could be as 'Self' which could be peculiar i.e. different from the usual or normal. Except Homo sapien being which is free from Voluptuousness, any other Voluptuous being of any sort couldn't be different from another Voluptuous being of same sort. Achieving this peculiarity could be possible for each and every Homo sapien being which is free from Voluptuousness. If any Player-'I' is peculiar, it will be clear that Player-'I' wouldn't have any quantity or quality of Voluptuousness. Then only, That Player-'I' could check and control Her'Self' means Her 'peculiarity' not to be affected or influenced by any other in any."

"Why could the checked and controlled only be educated ?"

"Without having one's own peculiarity, none could be educated by any of the Learned. It is to be noted that one could be imprisioned, tied or fettered but couldn't be controlled or checked. From childhood if one is imparted with traditions and customs of Lineage or Clan, for that one a lot of possibility would be there to be controlled or checked. Hence, the Tradition and the customs must be preserved by either Lineage or Clan or the Political State. The one, who isn't checked and controlled, couldn't be peculiar in any item of any subject. Because, the One who couldn't innovate one's peculiarity and behave accordingly, that one could do, act and behave as a Voluptuous being which could be tamed but can never be educated."

Chapter-40

"As You have told that to educate means to develop mentally, morally and aesthetically, to develop mentally means what ?"

"You have already been told that the Macro form of the Atman (the Soul) is the Mind. The Mind which is in all Voluptuous beings, could feel whereas The Mind, which is in Homo sapien beings could also feel like that of Voluptuous beings, in addition to feel, it could apply the Intellect which couldn't be graced upon the Voluptuous beings. To develop mentally means to instruct The Player-'I' or The Believer-in 'I' to feel for which and not to feel for which. Besides, make the Player-'I' or The Believer-in 'I' able think in a logical way. If the Mind of the Playe-'I' or The Believer-in 'I' is developed, either The Player-'I' or The Believer-in 'I' could feel when attended-deed is not proper to be adopted to observe the Practice and either The Player-'I' or The Believer-in 'I' could be able to think in a logical way to learn the reasons for not adopting properly. Therefore, either The Player-'I' or The Believer-in 'I' could know the spirit."

"To develop morally means ?"

" 'Moral' means how is a Homo sapien being to behave in a way that is considered right and good. The right is that which agrees with the Truth. So, the human being must do any thing which would be of the Truth i.e. The Only "I" means every each and every 'I' must do the thing which leads to learn that every each and every 'I' would be The Only "I" and to regain that 'Onlyness' of The Only "I". The good is that which doesn't affect or harm any. As the Player-'I' or The Believer-in 'I' must attend that deed resulting in The Player-

'I' or The Believer-in 'I' must not fall from the state at which at present The Player-'I' or The Believer-in 'I' would be there. Any attended-deed does not cause either The Player-'I' or The Believer-in 'I' to be fallen from the present 'State' or cause The Player-'I' or The Believer-in 'I' to invigorate from the present 'State' to higher 'State' would be the good. So, to develop morally means to do Right and good things."

"To develop aesthetically means ?"

"Aesthetic means study of the Beauty, the Art, the Literature and the Music. The Beauty is that which exalts the Mind pleasurably. The first and foremost quality of the Mind is to feel. The Mind would feel pleasurably when the being watches or views something which is beautiful. The something can be in any form. When the something can be in such form which could draw the attention of the being or hold up activities of a being that something will be said to have been beautiful. But this drawing the attention or that holding up activities which would not affect but must be pleasurable. Here, form means the essential natural of a thing or a person that determines its kind. The Art is that the conscious use of skill and creative imagination especially in the generating of aesthetic objects, in this regard, three words are to be learnt, one is the Skill which means ability to do something expertly and well that comes from the Practice. To copulate is also a skill, though, the sexual organs instinctively provoke to copulate. Only that Homo sapien being which doesn't have Voluptuousness can have 'Skill' to copulate. When both male Homo sapien being and female Homo sapien being are without Voluptuousness and do copulate each other, then only, they would gradually learn the Skill of copulating physically. The Physical copulation is physical copulation only though it is influenced by the

Mind. Though the Mind which would influence the Physical copulation as being felt or applying the Intellect, it would be the Physical copulation because in this copulation, the sense-pleasure would dominate the Mind. The difference between the copulation done by the Voluptuous beings and the Homo sapien beings which are free from Voluptuousness is that in the copulation done by the Voluptuous, the sense-pleasure would only be there whereas in the copulation done by the Homo sapien beings free from Voluptuous beings is the sense-pleasure along with mental pleasure. Owing to feel only sense-pleasure, a female Voluptuous being doesn't seek same male Voluptuous being to which it has just copulated or by which has just been copulated. At each and every time whenever it gets itself provoked to have copulation or it is got provoked by male Voluptuous being, it doesn't seek same male Voluptuous being it copulates or is copulated. Regarding to male Voluptuous being also, a male being too doesn't seek same female Voluptuous being to which it has just copulated or by which it has been provoked to copulate. Like female Voluptuous being, it would too be unaware of which female being it copulates to. When a male Homo sapien being and a female Homo sapien being behave like a male Voluptuous being and a female Voluptuous being, they could not be Homo sapien beings who have been graced upon the Skill which comes from the Practice meant to regain the Unlost. While the Practice being observed consistently, the Skill would be accustomed or mastered. When a male Homo sapien being is accustomed or mastered to the Skill and that Homo sapien being would physically copulate with a female Homo sapien being, the Mind of that Homo sapien being would feel that copulation and apply Intellect to do that physical copulation. When the Mind of that male Homo sapien being applies Intellect, that male Homo sapien being would do that physical copulation expertly and very well. At the same time the Mind of the female Homo sapien being which is copulated by that male Homo sapien being can feel that copulation and apply Intellect to do that copulation to be done expertly and very well. When the Mind of a male Homo sapien being does accordingly, then, that male Homo sapien being would seek same female Homo sapien being to which that male Homo sapien being has just physically copulated. In the case of the female Homo sapien being too, when the Mind of female Homo sapien being does like of male Homo sapien being, that female Homo sapien being would seek same male Homo sapien being by which it has been physically copulated. As long as the Skill of copulating physically, while the Minds of both male and female Homo sapien beings, do respond along with applying Intellect, is getting developed the same couple of male Homo sapien being and female Homo sapien being would wish to have copulation with each other. Thus, none of them would desire any other than each other. A couple of a male Homo sapien being and a female Homo sapien being do to seek each other, then, it can be check being done by their 'Selves' i.e. by His'Self' and Her'Self'. This check would control a Player-'I' to seek only one Believer-in 'I' to have copulation at each and every time whenever that Player-'I' do feel passion to have copulation and a Believer-in 'I' to seek only one Player-'I' to copulate at each and every time whenever that Believer-in 'I' do feel passion to have copulation. If this 'Check' is accustomed to a Player-'I' then, that Player –'I' could learn the gracing of the Believer-in 'I'. if this 'Check' is accustomed to a Believer –in 'I', then, that Believer-in 'I' could learn the worshipping of Player-'I' and grace Player-'I' accordingly. Only these Player-'I' and Believer-in 'I' could perform Mental Intercourse. The second word is imagination means to think of something in the Mind. As long as each and every 'I' am there in the 'Many' as each and every 'I' am only, every each and every 'I' would indwell in the body of Voluptuous being or Homo sapien being. But this each and every 'I' am two in sex i.e. The Player-'I' and The Believer-in 'I'. In course of Performing copulation, both male and female Homo sapien beings who are free from Voluptuousness could imagine that performance to be taken in various forms i.e. casting looks an each other, exchanging smiles and uttering elegant, refind, courtly, modish, fashionable and graceful words etc. This sort of performance must be own of The Player-'I' and The Believer-in 'I' i.e. both should not imitate other's own. So, both must imagine their own to perform. When a Player-'I' imitate any of another Player-'I', the spirit of Believer-in 'I' whom that Player-'I' seek wouldn't receive that Player-'I'. Alike, that Player-'I' would become unable to continue the performance with Believer-in 'I' who imitate any of another Believer-in 'I'. It is to be ever noted that the Intellect could be exerted to imagine. So, imagination must be possible to both male Homo sapien being and female Homo sapien being when they are free from Voluptuousness. When the imagination would be peculiar in respect of a Player-'I', that Player-'I' could be creative in every thing. Regarding the Believer-in 'I' also the same thing would be there. When a Player-'I' could imagine creatively or could be creative, that Player-'I' would be regarded to have the Art. Alike, a Believer-in 'I' could imagine creatively or could be creative, that Believer-in 'I' would also be regarded to have the Art. When The Player-'I' who would be regarded to have the Art and The Believer-in 'I' who would be regarded to have the Art and if that Player-'I' worship this Believer-in 'I' and this Believer-in 'I' grace this Player-'I', then only, the recondite entanglement to have mental intercourse would be united for them. Without awareness of their united recondite entanglement, they would immerse in mental intercourse. So, achieving the Art for them would be the most must-have."

Chapter-41

"What is that Art ?"

"The Dictionary gives the Meaning to the Art that the creation or expression of what is beautiful. It is to be noted and must be remembered in the Mind that the entire creation would be with three things which would be quite differed from one another. The first thing is the WORLD i.e. acronym of Water, Orb, Room, Light and Draught which are five basic or fundamental elements, the second thing is the Energy which would not be the WORLD but without WORLD this energy couldn't be deemed as being existed and the Third thing is the Art which would not contain the WORLD and would not be the Energy but without WORLD and ENERGY, it would not be visioned. When the Art is visioned by dint of the WORLD and the Energy it couldn't be beyond the entire creation like The Only "I". Though the Art would be so regarding with WORLD and ENERGY, it could not be The Only "I". As the Art would be perceptible to the Beings who would and could cause the Art to be deemed as being visioned. The 'Many', which has been come into existence due to the 'Will' done by The Only "I", which is addressed or called as the Creation, would also be the expression of what is beautiful. But this creation couldn't be taken granted for the creation or expression of what is beautiful which would be done by the Homo sapien being, in some cases, by the Voluptuous being. The 'Many' which is termed or called as the creation would be the sport of The Only "I" but not the creation or expression of what is beautiful which would be done by the Homo sapien being or the Voluptuous being. Because, the sport would be so which wouldn't be the skill acquired by the experience, the study or the observation etc. The Only "I" would be beyond all and would do 'Will' only to be 'Many'. Both the 'Will' and the 'Many' would be simultaneously done that too within the least duration to be reckoned in the second of which span of time couldn't be got to the Intellectuality. This 'Many' would contain each and every one who would have to be and go on during entire the 'Many' and each and every thing which would have to be and have to be done during entire the 'Many'. The Art would be skill acquires by experience, study or observation etc. Though, both The Sport of The Only "I" and the Art of any Homo sapien being or any Voluptuous being would look 'Unique', they would never be one and the same. Even each and every Art of each and every Homo sapien being and each and every Voluptuous being would not be one and the same. Though the Art of any being and the sport of The Only "I" wouldn't be one and the same and The Only "I" would be beyond the Art of every being and the sport of The Only "I" and The Only "I" would be the Art also. I narrate the Art in poetic manner too. Listen !

You could be felt, experienced, enjoyed, perceived and envisioned.

But You couldn't be seen, heard, tasted, smelt and touched.

All of You is clear and all of You are clear.

Those which sense all of You and all of You would remain functionless.

None could find You by means of and by dint of them.

You don't need such fulcrum which they need for their function.

Without that fulcrum none could experience You.

Truly You aren't comprised of any of that Fulcrum.

But they are certainly so.

While envision You they lose and ignore what they have and are.

Though they do, they need what they lose and ignore.

Thus You look beyond them but within them You don't be.

You are not alike for this one and that one.

For this You are done in some way and for that in some other.

Actually experience is same but experiencing of this and that differs from each other.

While You go on as You, neither doer nor doing subsists separately from each other.

But You exist apart from doer who couldn't after a while.

So only "I" am You also.

Here, You have to note that the speaker of this poem would be The Only "I" who would be beyond the 'Many' in which only the 'Art' could be found. The Only "I", in this poem, am addressing the Art. So, in this poem, 'You' stand for the 'Art' which can be sensed by the Homo sapien beings and in some cases by the Voluptuous beings too. But no Homo sapien being or Voluptuous being could find it. The Art could be seemed beyond all beings but without them it couldn't be there. The Art is so which is done for some in some way and for some other in some other way. But the Art exists apart from the Doer who leaves the body in which the Doer i.e. a Homo sapien being or a Voluptuous being indwells. The Doer leaves the body but the Art done by that Doer would remain. Hence it can be comprehended that though the Art is by the Doer, it could be seemed beyond all beings. So, the character to be beyond all would be had with the Art in some extent. To be beyond all would lead any to achieve the Ultimate end i.e. to be beyond the 'Many'. Therefore, The Only "I" who have been venerated as the speaker of this poem, conclude this poem by telling,

"I" am 'You' also.

Hence, each and every 'I' either 'I' may be The Player-'I' or The Believer-in 'I' must learn the Art to be done or to drink the Art already done. Doing the Art or drinking the Art done would transcend the Doer to be aesthetic."

Chapter-42

"What is Literature ?"

"Literature is all the writings of expression of permanent ideas for universal interest. This Literature could be in two sorts. One sort is the Literature in certain language i.e. Literature in English Language etc. and another sort is the Literature of certain thought i.e. The Eastern (Indian) Thought or The Western (Non-Indian) Thought. Now we have been dialoguing in English Language. So, our Dialogue, of which subject is from the Eastern side of the Earth, is in English Language. Hence, our Dialogue is the Eastern (Indian) Thought or The Eastern (Indian) Literature in English Language."

"When the subject of our Dialogue is from the Eastern side of the Earth, why would be dialoguing in English Language ?"

"To this Your question, I have already answered in poetic manner. Listen ! It seems You have not understand without having any doubt so I repeat so and take down it.

Education is manifestation of perfection existing in the human being already; Nothing could be remained as Existence ultimately.

Grammar is made as the Policy for things to be let in order like universes.

Letter innovate "I" as the letters that establish the letter is indestructible.

"I" ought to have been learnt as The Only "I" would be there ever.

Self is the subject that could stand for The Only "I".

Hour is certainly conceived as the Illusion at any cost indubitably.

Having been taken down, You note every first letter of every poetic line from top to bottom You can find the word, 'ENGLISH'. Have You found ?"

"Yes. I have. Then... ?"

"Then, comprehend the content of this poem. It certainly brings to the light that each and every one could be cozily educated by the language which would be available in the script written in letters. 1. So, the Language is the best source to educate each and every one. Actually Education, the Eastern (Indian) thought does preach, is manifestation of perfection existing in the human being already. In each and every being other than human being too the perfection is existing. But the being other than human being couldn't manifest the perfection and couldn't be trained or imparted to do so. Here, which or who would be the perfection ? The Answer would always be only one that The Only "I" who would be either The One or The Thing. Each and every 'I' would be too The Only "I", so, the perfection existing in the human being would be The Only "I". The Perfection existing in the Voluptuous being too would be The Only "I". But the human being can manifest this perfection i.e. envision The Only "I" whereas the Voluptuous being couldn't ever. 2. When The Only "I" do 'Will' 'Not to be Many', then, 'the entire Many' would mingle in The Only "I". Now this Only "I" would be 'Nothing' i.e. None of each and every 'I' and No thing of The Thing would be there. Hence, now this Only "I" would be there even this "I" couldn't be qualified by Only as now "I" would be only "Onlyness' which would be Nothing except this Nothing there would not be anything to have been. Hence it must be understood that Nothing stands for

Existence and Existence stands for Nothing. Thus it is crystal clear that genuinely Nothing would only exist. 3. The letter would be the sign of the sound which would express certain idea, content etc. By dint of letters in alphabet, all the ideology could be drawn. This drawn ideology would only be the letters i.e. The Literature of which ultimate goal is to envision the "I" i.e. The Only "I" which would be indestructible, hence, The Literature could also be indestructible. Therefore, each and every 'I' who am indwelling in the body of Homo sapien being ought to learn that indestructible The Only "I" by dint of the Literature. So, the subject of the Literature would be 'Self' i.e. each and every 'I' i.e. The Only "I". When the Day and the Night which could be taken granted for reckoning the Time, the Time would be revealed as the Illusion because as per revolvings and rotatings of the Earth only the Time is being reckoned. Actually the Time is neither a thing nor any item, at least, to be illusioned in 'the Many'. Thus, the Ideology or the content is from the Eastern (Indian) thought which has been expressed in English Language. Thus, the English Language is the best means to express the Easter thought along with Western Thought. The English Language is the so best means in which The Letter from the Alphabet, I, would sound The Only "I" who would be Only 'One'. This 'One' would be beyond during 'the Many', so, this would be 'One' only. And this 'One' would be only 'One' when there would be 'Not to be Many'. This would be the specificity of the English Language in which we have been dialoguing. The Letter, I in the Alphabet would be extolled allergorically while The Only "I" symbolically being represented in the Poetic manner. Listen !

'I' am a single lettered word.
'A' is also same
But 'A' is an adjective.

'I' stand for the 'Subject'
But 'A' qualifies it.

'I' even stand for the 'object'
In some other form.

But 'A' can't be changed
Into any other.

As I or some other form
I may be looked at,
uttered and sounded
As more than one.

But in form, sound and utterance
A is only A
However, it can't be away
From I.

When 'I' remain as only 'I'
Without giving any scope
To be envisioned by the 'Self',
Then no existence of 'A'
Is found.

All others comprise
More than one letter.
Single letter of any
Can never sound any
Each letter depends
On each other
Or one another.

The disorder of their comprisers
May make noise;
But can't sound as required.

'I' only don't require
Any order.
Because
Nothing is either side of me.

So 'I' am the Independent
In Truth, the Self-dependent
Of which entity
All can be possible.

Thus it is crystal clear that in English Language the letter 'I' gives the meaning to the person who is speaking. In the (Indian) Eastern Thought 'I' means The Only "I" who do the 'Will' to be 'many' and 'Not to be Many'. In the Eastern Language i.e. Sanskrit Language, the word, 'AHAM' means 'I' who stand for The Almighty who do create all i.e. from gods to beings and all universes which contain heavenly bodies such as the Space, the Sky, the Sun, the Stars, the Planets and the Satilites etc. In this poem 'I' am the letter 'I' who do speak. Both 'I' who am the letter in English Language and 'I' who would be The Only "I" would be Independent and The Self-dependent. Hence, we have been dialoguing the Eastern Thought in English Language. By dint of above two poems it has been crystal cleared that the Literature must be of The Only "I" who would be each and every one thing, though, The Only "I" would be beyond each and every one and thing. This Literature could be written in any Language either from The Eastern or The Western."

Chapter-43

"What is the Music ?"

"Music is not such word to which giving the meaning in single or few words is hardly possible. Even it couldn't be defined in single definition. 1. Music is an art of sound in Time that expresses ideas and emotions. If the words in a sentence or sentences are expressed rhythemetically, it can be surely accepted that those sentences contain the Music. Because these words or sentences would be pleasing or sweet sound. The Dictionary defines that the Music is science or art of ordering tones or sounds in succession, in combination and in temporal relationships to produce a composition having unity and continuity. The earliest hymns in this World i.e. on this Earth, which are said to be the earliest literature, too, are handed down to have been composed musically. Thus the Music is the part and parcel of the Literature in which the Language would command the Music for the idea, the content and the ideology to be expressed out whereas the Music would be contributory to the cause of the Literature. It can be assumed that the Literature and the Music would always be inseparable and undetachable twins. Any composed thing in writing without Music can be informative to those who observe the Practice meant to Regain the Unlost but not contributory to that Practice to be observed seriously and concentratedly. Actually the Music is a form of the Sound, the first and foremost item of the Matter would come into existence when The Only "I" do 'Will' to be 'Many'. Apart from every each and every 'I', for all forms which are said to be the forms of Energy in the Matter, The Form of the sound would be the basic form. The Sound would be fundamentally in two sorts. The first is that sort of sound which produces a sound i.e. noise and the second, is that sound which does have an implied meaning. The sort of Sound, which does have an implied meaning, could be a word, a sentence, a paragraph and the entire writing work in any aspect such as a dialogue, a hymn, a song, a story, a poem, a drama etc. Either The Only "I" or every each and every 'I' would be the Paramount and the Absolute meaning of the sound which does have the implied meaning. So, each and every 'I' who am observing the Practice must be alert in uttering the words from any literary aspects correctly, properly, exactly and without having the defect of mis-pronunciation, if not alert in doing, that utterance must affect the Practice. It is ever to be noted that though The Only "I" or every each and every 'I' would be beyond the entire Many, the implied Meaning of the Pronounced or the uttered word would be The Only "I" or every each and every 'I'. whenever the word is mis-pronounced or mis-uttered, the meaning of that mis-pronounciation or misutterance would always be in 'the Many' or of 'the Many' only. Because, The Only "I" or every each and every 'I' would never be prefixed or suffixed with any as The Only "I" and every each and every 'I' would be 'Onlyness' forever. Either The Only "I" or every each and every 'I' would be certainly qualified by the Adjective but in Nature couldn't be undoubtedly and decisively prefixed and suffixed by any. When either reading or singing is done with required rhythm, though the meaning of that reading or singing might be understood or not either reader or singer must be wrapped in that reading or singing. Owing to be wrapped up alike, the Reader or the Singer would assume the form of the sound i.e. the actual meaning of that Reading or that Singing. But this form which is assumed to that Reader or that Singer couldn't be imperceptible even to that Reader or that Singer too. The Thing which is imperceptible is a form of The Only "I" who would be imperceptible to any in 'the

Many'. Hence, that Reader or that Singer who has assumed the form which couldn't be imperceptible is said to have been in the right path to Regain the Unlost. Therefore, to educate means to develop mentally, morally and aesthetically. One, who has developed mentally, could feel that for which one would have to do and be able to think in logic way. It is here to be noted that Feeling and Thinking would be done in the 'Many' only, beyond 'the Many' neither Feeling nor Thinking would be necessary. One, who has developed morally, could behave in a way that is considered right which is said to have agreed with the Truth that is Preached to be the first character of The Only "I". It is always kept in the Heart and on the Mind that Developing mentally and morally could be ultrapractically useful to the Practitioner to expedite the Practice to Regain the Unlost. But the One, who has developed mentally, morally along with aesthetically, could assume the imperceptible form, which is authoritatively or horonifically stated to be the state of congeniality between The Only "I" and the One i.e. each and every 'I' who observe the Practice meant to Regain the Unlost."

Chapter-44

"What is the Congeniality?"

"The congeniality means having the same nature and the power of transferal to the care or possession of another and the same tastes."

"Can both The Player-'I' and The Believer-in 'I' attain the same nature ?"

"The first and foremost step or stage of the Practice meant to Regain the Unlost is to attain the same nature only. The same Nature could be attained."

"How ?"

"When The Player-'I' honestly, sincerely and devotedly do worship The Believer-in 'I' whom The Player-'I' have opted or selected and The Believer-in 'I' who could with affection notice honest, sincere and devoted doing of worship being done by The Player-'I' who have opted or selected The Believer-in 'I' and instinctively i.e. without having supposition or pre-occupied opinion The Believer-in 'I' do grace The Player-'I', then, that Player-'I' would be hymned and this Believer-in 'I' would be lauded. Thus The Player-'I' could arrive at the stage from which The Player-'I' couldn't be fallen from and The Believer-in 'I' tender heartedly would condescend to the stage at which The Player-'I' have arrived or could spontaneously arrive at the stage from which The Player-'I' have arrived. Accordingly both The Player-'I' and The Believer-in 'I' could sojourn at the stage for a long as 'Two on One and One in Two'. This sojourning would be esteemed as same Nature."

"How long sojourning can be ?"

"Until both The Player-'I' and The Believer-in 'I' could learn The Spirit which would be One in both The Player-'I' and The Believer-in 'I'."

"During the Period of sojourning of The Player-'I' and The Believer-in 'I', how do The Player-'I' and The Believer-in 'I' do, act and behave ?"

"In this period, The Player-'I' wouldn't have own conscious of The Player-'I', The Player-'I' do each and every deed pertaining to the Materialistic World not for The Player-'I' but for The Believer-in 'I'. The Player-'I' would prepare food to the taste of The Believer-in 'I' who would have it without sensing the taste of it but to extend the gratitude for the healthy and salutary food prepared to keep the Sanity of The Believer-in 'I' up. When The Player-'I' would have sincere intention that the food must be prepared to the physical health and the Sanity of The Player-'I' and The Believer-in 'I' would have it while extending gratitude for the felicitous service rendered in this regard, the Intention and gratitudeness of both get transferred into each other. Hence, Both The Player-'I' and The Believer-in 'I', though differ in terms of physical bodies from each other ; would infuse into the Minds of each other. So, some extent, the Minds of The Player-'I' and The Believer-in 'I' would become one and the same. Therefore both The Player-'I' and The Believer-in 'I' could feel alike in response to any and express same in same words in same style simultaneously though both would be on the same spot or at the different places without learning where they would be. The Listener would listen same words or in same style simultaneously with same idea in different tones and voices. The Listener could listen to same words in same style asynchronously too with same idea in different tones and voices. When if it so happens to the Listener to listen those words from The Player-'I' and The Believer-in 'I' at different places and at different time or same time. No Listener could up hold whose words would actually be those and who would resonate whose words. The Player-'I' wouldn't observe prejudicial outlook towards the relatives such as parent, brother, sister of The Believer-in 'I' but receive and treat them that of The Player-'I'. Even The Player-'I' wouldn't secern in any thing in any manner on any time between consanguineous Kin of The Player-'I' and The Believer-in 'I'. If in ineluctable circumstances The Player-'I' is put to test, The Player-'I', without second thought, would select the consanguineous Kin of The Believer-in 'I' as the consanguineous Kin of The Player-'I'. The same love, affection, affinity, respect, regard, honour, uprightness, treatment etc. Which The Player-'I' would extend to consanguineous Kin of The Player-'I' must be extended, beyond doubt, by The Player-'I' to those of The Believer-in 'I' in same manner. Thus The Player-'I' wouldn't give any scope for sojourning couldn't be affected for little span of time too. The Player-'I' Would only have to worship The Believer-in 'I', so, The Player-'I' would have to do the Practice along with The Believer-in 'I' in what place The Believer-in 'I' would reside. Therefore The Player-'I' would receive all of The Believer-in 'I' as of The Player-'I'. The Believer-in 'I' would also have to treat and receive all of The Player-'I' as of The Believer-in 'I'. Keeping sojourning would be of both The Player-'I' and The Believer-in 'I'. 3. On being wedded auspiciously, both The Player-'I' and The Believer-in 'I' would achieve the martial status. So, they lead martial life and gradually mould that life to strengthen their Practice meant to Regain the Unlost. During the earliest period of their wedded life, both would lead each life as lives of The Player-'I' and The Believer-in 'I', gradually both could mould their lives which may as two lives into the Life which couldn't be conspicuous as two to the eye or the Mind of those who could follow them at each and every second. All the Voluptuous beings could lead their lives but only the Homo sapien beings, if free from Voluptuousness, could mould their lives as the Life. To mould lives into the Life, both The Player-'I' and The Believer-in 'I' would have to take so many decisions or make policies either in no time or on time or in time or against time or at the same time or from time to time or at times or at all times or at other times or time and again or many a time or at the best of times. Thus both The Player-'I' and The Believer-in 'I' would crossover and surpass each other."

"Crossing over and surpassing each other ! How ?"

"During the state of sojourning, The Player –'I', while attending or doing all deeds for which The Player-'I' would be to do, would gradually become the learned to have known the Beingness which level or range that Player-'I' have when The Player-'I' entered into the 'Many' come into existence by the 'Will' which The Only "I" do. As Learned own Beingness of The Player-'I', The Player-'I' would attend or do deeds intended to envision that Beingness without outer consciousness that could be expressed in words or in any languages that contain any signs other than words. In the course of doing such deeds, The Player-'I' would conceive that Playe-'I' don't have absolute level or range of Beingness but some and remaining level or range of Beingness would have been had with The Believer-in 'I'. So, The Player-'I' would make all efforts with best for Beingness of The Player-'I' to be merged into the Beingness of The Believer-in 'I'. For this merging only, The Player-'I' would ignore Her'Self'. Thus ignoring Her'Self', The Player-'I' would reach the ultimate stage of the worship. At this stage of worship, the worshipper would never claim anything in return or requital etc. But The Player-'I' must deserve to be rewarded at least. During this state of sojourning, The Believer-in 'I', while keeping the doing meant to keep the Beingness, would gradually become the Learned to have known the Doingness which level or range That Believer-in 'I' have when The Believer-in 'I' entered into the same 'Many'. As Learned own Doingness of The Believer-in 'I', The Believer-in 'I' would attend or do deeds intended to envision that Doingness without consciousness that could be expressed in words or in any languages that contain any signs other than words. In the course of doing such deeds, The Believer-in 'I' would conceive that The Believer-in 'I' don't have absolute level or range of Doingness but some and remaining level or range of Doingness would have been had with The Player-'I'. So, The Believer-in 'I' would make all efforts with best for the Beingness of The Player-'I' to be merged with the Beingness of The Believer-in 'I'. To fill in the blank of the Beingness of The Believer-in 'I' with the Beingness of The Player-'I',The Believer-in 'I' would do as the Doer like The Player-'I' whose ignoring of 'Self' would be nothing but learning 'Self' would be 'the Self' of The Playing –'I' and The Believing-in 'I'. Here Learning 'Self' means being as 'The Self'; and filling in the blank of Beingness means being as 'The Doer'. It is to be kept on Mind and in Heart that 'The Self' and 'The Doer' are though, one and the same, both would have identity of each separately and each of them would cross over and surpass other. As the Doer, The Believer-in 'I' would deify The Player-'I' who would have been worshipping The Believer-in 'I'. While deifying The Player-'I', The Believer-in 'I' would go on treating The Player-'I' as a goddess though That Player-'I' wouldn't have charm or be beauty in physical appearance. The Believer-in 'I' would not watch whether The Player-'I' would be either eyeful or fascinating or honey or stunner or not. Instead, The Believer-in 'I' would watch ingenuous feelings in the eyes, sanctity in the fascinating expressions, literal meaning in all honeying words being uttered and as stunner when inconceivable cooperation extends in each activity. Owing to this watching as the Doer, The Believer-in 'I' cross over The Player-'I'. The Player-'I' wouldn't pause the doing of worshipping of The Believer-in 'I' for the least span. Instead, The Player-'I' would pause the worshipping The Believer-in 'I' to receive each and every watching of The Believer-in 'I' who would do towards The Player-'I' who would invite each and every items of The Believer-in 'I'. The Believer-in 'I' would acknowledge this invitation as the grace of The Player-'I'. Thus The Player-'I' would be honoured without the knowledge of The Player-'I' as The Player-'I' would cross over The Believer-in 'I'."

"Owing to crossing over each other, what would happen ?"

"The Player-'I' would learn that The Player-'I' would have been worshipping The Self of The Player-'I' only in form of The Believer-in 'I'. This learning would make The Player-'I' know that 'I' would be in Two who would be The Player-'I' and The Believer-in 'I'. Therefore, The Player-'I' would worship The Believer-in 'I' while considering worshipping of The Believer-in 'I' as worshipping of The Player-'I' only. The Believer-in 'I' would grace The Player-'I' while considering gracing upon The Player-'I' as gracing upon The Believer-in 'I' only. Thus, The Doingness of The Player-'I' would gradually merge into the Beingness of The Player-'I', alike, The Beingness of The Believer-in 'I' would enable The Doingness to be engrossed in The Beingness of The Believer-in 'I'."

Chapter-45

"At this stage, both The Player-'I' and The Believer-in 'I' do achieve what ?"

"At this stage only, Love Making (Making Love) could be possible."

"Could You please narrate it ?"

"Yes. In a poem, it could be done. Listen to it.

Actually who does enjoy and who is enjoyed ?
Though it could not be done by only One,
It seems that Doer is only One in that both,
Another one is inferred as enjoying doing.

It looks one does make another one enjoy in
That in which another one too looks as if
Another one did make one enjoy like another
One or as one does wish from another one.

It couldn't be possible to make out clearly
Whose is doing and whose is wishing even
Both one and another one could not as well
Express or tell what part each played in it.

Even both they couldn't endorse either each
Participating or cooperating each other in it
Whenever they take part to do or to be done
To submit each other to enjoy each other.

In the end of their submission to each other,
Both they would remain as they would thank
To each other for adoring each other as no
Sense pleasure flashed in that 'love making'."

"Oh ! If it so happen, it would be prodigious wonder. Really unbelievable. What does enjoy mean ?"

"Enjoy means experiencing something which is good."

"What would be experienced ? And how is it good for that both ?"

"To experience 'Love' being cast from the Mind while applying Intellect would be something. Both Minds would respond while casting 'Love'. When the 'Love' is cast, no applying Intellect will be needed. But Intellect would be applied instinctively not to let sense-pleasure arise. The Intercourse in which, though sexual-organs participate, no sense-pleasure would arise but 'Love' would cast and be experienced equitably in quality and quantity would be cognized as Mental Intercourse. As the Love would be Vital in this Mental Intercourse, this Mental Intercourse would be designated as 'Love Making'."

"What would happen, if sense-pleasure arises ?"

"Then, one of both would feel enjoying that Intercourse and another one would feel being enjoyed by one and enjoy one's enjoying."

"What would be wrong with one and another one, if one and another one do feel so ?"

"If one does feel, within no time one would fall from that state of Love Making and would be for the commotion felt by another one who would be still at that state of Love-Making. So does one."

"Are both Doers or is one of both Doers there in the Love Making ?"

"Any someone other than one or another one could never answer to this question. Even that one and Another one who would be in Love Making could not answer to this question even after completion of their Love Making."

"But in the poem it is asserted that 'It seems that doer is only one in that both'. Doesn't this poetic line infer there is one doer only ?"

"It isn't an assertion. So only verb 'Seems' is used in the main clause. But it can be inferred as an assertion as well."

"Why can't it be taken as assertion ?"

"During the Copulation i.e. physical intercourse, the Penis of The Believer-in 'I' enters into the Vagina of The Player-'I' and gives strokes. This striking is also done in Love Making. In copulation, it is no doubt, The Believer-in 'I' would be a doer as The Believer-in 'I' would give strokes and The Player-'I' would receive strokes or would be enjoyed by means of strokes. No doubt, The Player-'I' too would enjoy the receiving strokes. But The Believer-in 'I' would be predominant. So it is clear that here the doer is The Believer-in 'I'. But in Love Making, both The Believer-in 'I' and The Player-'I' would equitably receive strokes and be equally enjoyed by each other."

"Would The Player-'I' too give strokes ?

"Physically it wouldn't be possible. Receiving the strokes of The Believer-in 'I' would be translated into giving the strokes while both are in Love Making. Correspondingly, enjoying the strokes given by The Believer-in 'I' would be translated into giving the strokes while both are in Love Making."

"Though the strokes given by The Believer-in 'I', The Believer-in 'I' wouldn't be the Doer and The Player-'I' wouldn't be enjoyed even none of both wouldn't be enjoyer as there would be translations. Would any of both be ?"

"You have just mistaken what is told. Here The Believer-in 'I' would give strokes to The Player-'I' but being received what would be given The Player-'I' would translate strokes as so to be received by The Believer-in 'I'. Thus, both would receive the strokes and enjoy them also. Hence, it couldn't be characterized that who would be the Doer and who would be the Enjoyer in Love Making."

"So, It could be endorsed that no question of sense-pleasure would be in Love Making ?"

"Yes. No question would be there."

"How long do both The Believer-in 'I' and The Player-'I' go on in that Love-Making ?"

"Until both reach The Spiritual Intercourse, they go on in that Love-Making."

"Can it be possible to any couple of The Believer-in 'I' and The Player-'I' to go on in Love-Making ?"

"Surely, it could be possible to that couple which quantifies never enjoying the lust being generated whenever their sexual-organs would copulate. It would never suppose to make sexual-organs copulate would be only intercourse. They would prefer their Minds with Intellect only in intercourse to their sexual organs. Thus they wouldn't need exerting their sexual organs to be in Love Making and go on in Love Making until they reach The Spiritual Intercourse."

"Do they get such stamina to be in Love Making at each and every second ?"

"No question of stamina to be in Love Making. Because Love Making would be of the Mind but not of physical bodies."

"You mean, for Love Making, it isn't necessary to let sexual organs participate in intercourse ?"

"Not always necessary. For the least span too not necessary. Without having their conscious their sexual organs would be let to participate."

"Can Love Making be possible when their sexual organs don't participate ?"

"Yes. possible, without having been touched by each other both The Believer-in 'I' and The Player-'I' can participate in Love Making."

"How ?"

"The Believer-in 'I' and The Player-'I' would use to be alert while never uttering or accepting in dream too

that each and every 'I' would be so who would be other than The Only "I";

that each and every 'I' ought to beg or pray The Only "I" to

bless each and every 'I' to be freed from all the bondages

instead facing all expostulation.

that both The Believer-in 'I' and The Player-'I' have the

Beingness which would be one and the same in The Believer-in

'I' and The Player-'I' that the level or range of the Beingness would be same in The Believer-in 'I' and The Player-'I'.

that the level or range of the Beingness would be same in The

Believer –in 'I' and The Player –'I' .

that the level or range of the Beingness in The Believer-in 'I'

would be not higher than that of which in The Player-'I'.

that the level or range of the Beingness in The Player-'I' would

not be lesser than that of which in The Believer-in 'I'.

that the total level or ranges of the Beingness in both The

Believer-in 'I' and The Player-'I' would never be in toto.

that both The Believer-in 'I' and The Player-'I' have the

Doingness which would be one and the same in The Believer-in

'I' and The Player-'I'.

that the level or range of the Doingness would be same in The

Believer-in 'I' and The Player-'I'.

that the level or range of the Doingness in The Player-'I' would

not be higher than that of which in The Believer-in 'I'.
that the level or range of the Doingness in The Believer-in 'I'

would not be lesser than that of which in The Player-'I'.

that the total levels or ranges of the Doingness in both The

Believer-in 'I' and The Player-'I' would never be in toto.

So, both The Believer-in 'I' and The Player-'I' would ever suppose that regarding Beingness, The Believer-in 'I' and The Player-'I' have been existing since beginninglessness and would have existing upto endlessness. Both wouldn't suspect the affinity that makes both suited to each other. This affinity would be rather than bonding. Hence, without having been touched by each other, both The Believer-in 'I' and The Player-'I' participate in Love-Making."

"How can another one notice that both The Believer-in 'I' and The Player-'I' have reached the state or the stage in which that both could be in Love-Making for which participating of sexual organs isn't necessary ?"

"View the scene displayed in the words of The Believer-in 'I' and The Player-'I' uttered separately during which situation both are away from each other. So that they couldn't have listened to each other.

'Oh ! My Lord could be at present free from all tensions or agonies or apprehensions or turmoiles etc. as all the items of his job were

successfully completed by last night'.

'Oh ! Last night I had slept with my Virtuous wife and went into dead

sleep. Now I am free from all tensions, agonies, apprehensions and

turmoils as I could have completed all the items of my job by the last

night. So, I have to have big-millet bread with two vegitable curries of

Bean and Bryonia.'

'Now I have to take at ten leaves of big-millet bread along with Bean

curry and Bryonia curry.'

'During this season Mango-fruits are produced. My beloved virtuous

wife can prepare Mango juice for me. But after having breakfast I will

have apples instead of Mango juice.'

'In this happiest mood of My Lord, it is better to give apples instead of

Mango juice to him after his having breakfast. Inveterately, he would

be engaged on his job after having breakfast. But today I have to

notify him to play chess with me for an hour. Later on, let him engage

on his job.'

'After having my breakfast, I will have to ask my Virtuous wife to play

chess with me for an hour. Later on, I will engage on my job.'

"Wow ! How could it have been possible to them to express same feelings out while they were away from each other ?"

"In Love-Making, the Partaking of The Minds of both could be sacrosanct. You are already known that The Mind would be Macro form of The Atman (The Soul) which would be free from all and one and the same in each and every Believer-in 'I' and each and every Player-'I'. Therefore, The Mind would, in true, be only one. When each and every 'I' would cherish the Illusion as each and every 'I' would be away from The Only "I", since then, The Mind would be deluded as Minds which would be separated from one another. When The Mind would be One, there wouldn't be either differed opinions or dissimilar assumptions."

Chapter-46

"To know and learn that Minds is the delusion but The Mind would be one and the same, what should I do ?"

"You must comprehend that just before the End of Your practice meant to Regaining the Unlost You must merge all Your 'Doingness' into Your 'Beingness'."

"How ? How could I do so ?"

"You must know and learn that 'Doingness' would be the form of the 'Beingness'."

"As You have just told, I can believe that 'Doingness' would be the form of the 'Beingness'. But how can I know it ?"

"When The Only "I" have done 'Will', since then only, You could have been Yourself speaking to Your 'self' as You i.e. each and every 'I'. Speaking to Your 'self' as You would only be Your 'beingness'. Thus as You, You are being followed by 'Be' form i.e. 'Are'. If You don't seem as You are in existence, then, 'Are' wouldn't follow You. The verb 'Be' or its form would disclose that One or Another one or Thing or Another thing would be there. You might have already held that You would be, in true, The Only "I" but cherished the Illusion that You would have been 'some' other than The Only "I". Your such cherishing has caused The verb 'Be' to get form, 'Are' for You. Actually, The Only "I" would be the 'Be' and so be The Only "I". What would be said to have been that would be The Only "I". Hence, The Only "I" would be the 'Be' and the 'Be' would The Only "I". The cherishing would be the first and foremost 'Doing' of which immediate doing would be getting from of 'Be', 'Are'. So, You must know and learn that as You, You have only done, 'Cherishing' at first. Cherishing would mean 'doing' something. Earlier than cherishing, there was not any kind of doing. Though the 'Be' is supposed as the verb, earlier cherishing of each and every 'I', the verb 'Be', in true, not the 'Be' because the verb 'Be' did not do any thing. Actually the Verb 'Be' do not do anything and did not do anything too. Meticulously, You must learn or commit to memory that when there is the 'Be', there would positively be the 'Do'. But the 'Do' could be made unexisted. Therefore, the 'Do' would be merged into the 'Be'. Hence it would be crystal clear that the 'Do' would emit from the 'Be'."

"How ?"

"Don't interrupt me. Let me continue. As You have been just told that The Only "I" would be the 'Be' and the 'Be' would be The Only "I", until The Only "I" do 'Will' to be 'Many', there wouldn't be each and every 'I'. When The Only "I" do 'Will' to be 'Many', all each and every 'I' would emerge; like-wise when The Only "I" do 'Will' to be Many since then only the forms of the 'Be' i.e. Am for I, Are for You and Is for He, She and It and Was for I, He, She and It and were for You would emit. Hence it would be crystal clear that the 'Do' would emit from the 'Be'. That which can be emitted from some, that emitted thing would ever be the form of its source. If not, no thing could ever come into existence as a thing."

"What is the difference between the forms of the 'Be' i.e. Am, Was, Are, Were and Is and the form i.e. 'Do'."

"The forms of 'Be' i.e. Am, Was, Are, Were and Is would be for I, You, He, She and It what the 'Be', Be for The Only "I". But another form i.e. the 'Do' would do what I, You, He, She and It do as each and every 'I' whereas The Only "I" don't do."

"Then... What would do 'Will' of The Only "I" be ?"

"Doing 'Will' of The Only "I" would never be the 'Do' of The Only "I" as The Only "I" would never be the Doer."

"Then, do Will of The Only "I" would mean what ?"

"The Only "I" do 'Will' i.e. suppose the 'Will'. But Doing i.e. supposing the Will and supposed 'Will' would be done simultaneously. For Time, there wouldn't be possible to exist or pass between Doing the 'Will' and the 'Will. Hence Doing which is being pointed out or noticed before the 'Will' as 'Do' would not be the 'Do' which follows the 'Be' forms of I, You, He, She and It."

"Then what would be actual difference between the 'Be' which can be the 'Verb' and the Verb, Do ?"

"You have already been told. I once again tell You that in simple present or past tense sentences for other contractions, the 'Be' would be only the Verb and wouldn't take even itself as an auxiliary verb whereas the 'Do' would take itself as so. There can be possible for 'Don't be late' etc. In this kind of sentences it must be understood 'Don't be' would be negative for 'Be' not 'do' i.e. Verb of subject of sentence."

"Yes, I have recollected which You are just telling. So what ?"

"So, the 'Be' would be independent, free, unique and absolute."

"How could the 'Be' be treated as 'independent' ?"

"Because, it would be both Main verb and Auxiliary verb."

"How could the 'Be' regarded as 'free'?"

"Because, in simple contractions the 'Be' would itself make sentence as interrogative too."

"How could the 'Be' assumed as 'unique' ?"

"Because, except the 'Be', all other verbs including the 'Do' would have similarities in many things. Besides, the 'Be' or forms of the 'Be' i.e. Am, Are, Is, Was and Were indicate the state of the subject whereas the 'do' indicates various actions of the subject. Hence, the verb 'Be' does never mean to do any (subject) but to be (subject)."

"What have You especially mentioned 'including the Do' ?"

"Because, regarding forms of basic verb, present and past participle of verb there would be some similarity between 'Be' and 'Do' as Be, Being and Been and Do, Doing and Done. But for past form, the 'Be' would be past in its forms only. It means there would never be the past for the 'Be' i.e. no past time for the 'Be' it means the 'Be' would ever be beyond the Time. Whereas the 'Do' would have the past form i.e. Did."

"So what ?"

"What there would be the Past for anything, it would be crystal clear that thing gets finished i.e. would lose its existence. Therefore, the 'Do' must merge into the 'Be' which would never lose its existence though it can be taken granted for verb."

"But You have told that when The Only "I" do 'Will', since then, "I" will be. Before 'Will' have been done by The Only "I", where the 'Be' had been ?"

"Before 'Will' have been done by The Only "I", there would not have had any difference, distinction, divergence, deviation or variance between The Only "I" and The 'Be'."

"How could You tell that there would not be such difference etc. ?"

"In Truth, The Only "I" would be The 'Be' and so would be The Only "I". So only there would be the Being which would stand for each and every 'I'. 'Be' stands for the 'Be' i.e. existence and 'ing' means going on. Hence, 'Being' means 'going on of existence'. The each and every 'I' who would be only The Only "I" who would be The Existence i.e. the 'Be' would exist i.e. go on during the 'Many' comes owing to 'Will' done by The Only "I". keeping in view of going on of each and every 'I' during the 'Many', each and every 'I' am being termed as 'Being'."

"Yes. I have recollected entire matter pertaining to the 'Being'. How could the 'Be' be absolute ?"

"No 'Be No 'Do'. As long as the 'Be' be there, the 'Do' could be there. But for the 'Be' to be, the 'Do' couldn't do anything though the 'Do' would stand for 'do'. So, the 'Be' only the absolute."

Chapter-47

"Wouldn't Merging of 'Doingness' into 'Beingness' be the Doing ?"

"Yes. It would ever be unbiased. Merging of Doingness into Beingness would be the Doing."

"Then, How could the Doing be finished ?"

"Remember ! Don't forget that 'Ing' would go on forever or forevermore."

"You mean ?"

" 'ing' stands for going on i.e. continuity. 'Be' goes on forever, so only, 'Being'. Hence, The Only "I" would be 'the being' i.e. each and every 'I'."

"Then, why wouldn't 'Do' go on as the Doing ?"

"The 'Be' i.e. The Only "I" do 'Will' whereas the Doer i.e. each and every 'I' do the 'Deed'."

"What is the difference between 'Will' and 'Deed' ?"

"Deed would be deemed as something done for a reward or a retribution. Without applying the Mind no each and every 'I' do 'Will'. Hence, receiving a reward or a retribution would depend upon the Mind."

"Could any 'Deed' be done without 'Will' which is done by applying the Mind ?"

"No 'Deed' could be done without 'Will'."

"Then, how could 'Will' be differed from 'Deed' ?"

" 'Will' could be done by 'Self' for self whereas 'Deed' for selfish."

"How ?"

"Who would You be ? You know well You would be each and every 'I' who am in Truth, The Only "I". The Only "I" do 'Will' to be Many not for The Only "I" but each and every 'I' who am striving, struggling and grieving to be The Only "I" from generations to generation even 'To be Many' to 'To be Many'. But as an each and every 'I', You do will many a time to achieve something while cherishing the Illusion that something could be something only but would not be The Only "I". This 'do' would cause each and every 'I' to go on doing something or something else. But 'do' will of The Only "I" wouldn't be a 'do' which each and every 'I' do. Hence, 'Will', like The Only "I" do, could be done by 'Self' which would stand for The Only "I" and 'Deed', like each and every 'I' do to achieve something which is deemed as separate from The Only "I", would be done for selfish of the doer."

"How could 'I' merge my 'Doingness' into 'Beingness' which would be at somewhere ?"

"So, You are still under impact of Illusion."

"So am 'I' ?"

"Resolutely, You are so. Neither confirmation nor ratification nor authentication nor substantiation nor testimony nor verification is required in this regard."

"How could You reach such resolution ?"

"As You have already been told that each and every 'I' would be a 'Being' and each and every 'I' would have such level and range of Beingness actually which would be inseparable and indivisible among all of each and every 'I' and between each and every 'I' and The Only "I", You are now inquiring 'Beingness' would be at somewhere."

Chapter-48

"Yes. I have been already told. How would I have said ?"

"You are still under impact of cherishing the Illusion that You would be separated from The Only "I"."

"Must not 'I' cherish that both The Only "I" and I would be separated from each other ?"

"As long as You do so, You could never know and learn The Truth that there would be The only 'One' which would be taken The Thing granted for The One done for."

"What would be that ?"

"That would be so that would be only in Existence from beginingless to endlessness. So, that could be honoured as The 'Be' i.e. That is only 'Be' which would be the First and foremost basic verb than all other verbs."

"You have told that The Only "I" would be in existence from beginningless to endlessness. Would both The 'Be' and The Only "I" be one and the same ?"

"Yes. There You are."

"Then, why would two concepts i.e. The 'Be' and The Only "I" be there for only 'One' or 'Thing'?"

"Until The Only "I" do 'Will' to be 'Many', there wouldn't be possible for any concept."

"Before The Only "I" have done 'Will', how could such One or Thing have been addressed or called ?"

"To be addressed or called no other one or thing was not there for One or Thing. Even One or Thing would not also call or address to Oneself or Thingself (Itself)."

"Wouldn't One or Thing stand for The Only "I" ?"

"In Truth, One or Thing would only be The Only "I" who have done 'Will' to be 'Many'. After 'Many' have been come into existence, One or Thing have started to address or call Oneself or Thingself (Itself) as "I" who would only be The Only "I"."

"So, "I" would be the concept to be addressed by The Only "I" to The Only "I". Then, what about the 'Be' ?"

"I am sure You have got cleared regarding the concept, "I"."

"Yes. I have. Then-?"

"The concept, "I" would be actually the pronoun for The 'Be' which would stand for One or Thing which would be only in Existence from the beginningless to the endlessness. You have been already told that the 'Be' would be the first and foremost basic verb."

"Yes. I have been told. So what ?"

"I am again sure that You have learnt each and every 'I' who have come into existence would be The Only "I"."

"Yes. I have learnt so. Then what ?"

"You have beyond doubt learnt that each and every 'I' would be The Only "I" and The Only "I" would be each and every 'I'. So, each and every 'I' could be taken as a form of The Only "I" granted for."

"In view of 'Many', The Only "I" would only be each and every 'I' as 'many' in number. So, all of each and every 'I' could be forms of The Only "I". So…?"

"Alike The Only "I", the 'Be' would be in forms such as 'am', 'are', 'is', 'was' and 'were. So, there was no past tense-form for the 'Be'."

"What about 'was' and 'were' ?"

" 'Was' is the past tense form of 'am' and 'is' and 'were' is the Past tense form of 'are'."

"Aren't 'was' and 'were' past tense forms of the 'Be' ?"

"Never. For each verb, there would be only one Past tense form. For example 'did' for 'do' and 'had' for 'have' etc."

"Why would the 'Be' be as so ?"

"Because, the 'Be' would be beginningless to endlessness. It means the 'Be' would be beyond Time. For the 'Be', no Time-sense could be expressed, inferred or sounded whenever 'be' is pronounced."

"Then what about 'Will be' etc. ?"

"Very keenly or exuberantly or fervidly if You learn, You could be aware of that pure auxiliary verb will only express, infer or sound Future Time-sense. The Main verb be would always be static."

"Then, what about other pure auxiliary verbs ?"

"Any other pure auxiliary verb could replace will in terms of sense rather than Time. All other pure auxiliary verbs would express, infer and sound 'Futurity'."

"You mean the 'Be' would never infer, express or sound Futurity. Don't You ?"

"Yes. I mean. This is not what I mean i.e. not interpretation of my choice. This is The Truth. The Past Time would be there. But The Future could be looked to be, but no certainty for the Future."

"No certainty ! Not be it there ?"

"Only Deed, Intention lies behind deed, Expectation from deed done or being done and Aspiration being arisen from deed would cause for The Future. If they aren't, no Future could be befallen."

Chapter-49

"But, though there wouldn't be deed, intention lies behind deed, expectation from deed done or being done and aspiration being arisen from deed, there could be possible for next second after present second is elasped. Could not be so ?"

"When there is neither effect nor aftermath nor consequence nor upshot nor affect nor bear upon nor impinge upon nor influence nor interest nor involvement nor prevailing upon nor transform nor aftereffect nor outcome nor result nor development nor sequel etc.., then, The Time i.e. next-second couldn't be possible to be elasped though the next-second is befallen."

"What would be the effect of the Deed ?"

"When the Deed is done, something can be come into force. So, the Doer would be held for that which comes into force."

"What would be the aftermath of the Deed ?"

"When the Deed is done, something can be affected. If that effect is an unpleasant, then, the Doer would be held for that aftermath."

"What would be the consequence of the Deed ?"

"When the Deed is done, something can be brought about. If that brought out causes to happen something to be ruined, the Doer would be held for that ruin. Sometimes this brought out causes to happen something to be restored. For this restoration too, the Doer would be held."

"What would be the affect of the Deed ?"

"When the Deed is done, something can be acted on. So, the Doer would be held for that which acts on someone or something."

"What would be the bearing upon of the Deed ?"

"When the Deed is done, some other thing can be relevant to something. So, the Doer would be held for some other thing which is borne upon something."

"What would be the impinge upon of the Deed ?"

"When the Deed is done, something can be made an impact upon. So, the Doer would be held for that something which is impinged upon."

"What would be the influence of the Deed ?"

"When the Deed is done, the character of someone can have an effect on. So, the Doer would be held for some one who is influenced. Whatever influence may be it, the Doer would have to undergo its consequence as a rule."

"What would be the interest of the Deed ?"

"When the Deed is done, someone can be given one's attention to something or some other one. So, the Doer would be held for giving one's attention to. Whichever thing or whoever some other one may be, either merited or demerited, the Doer would be held for that giving to."

"What would be the involvement of the Deed ?"

"When the Deed is done, something or someone can be got into a complicated condition. So, the Doer would be held for that complication."

"What would be the prevailing upon of the Deed ?"

"When the Deed is done, someone can be persuaded to do something. Whatever something done may be, the Doer would be held to share in."

"What would be the transform of the Deed ?"

"When the Deed is done, something can be changed. So, the Doer would be held for that transformation of shape, quality, appearance or character etc."

"What would be the aftereffect of the Deed ?"

"When the Deed is done, something can be effected which occurs afterwards. It means in some cases, something doesn't come into effect immediately. It must be done later. Here, later could be applied for next incarnation, incarnation comes after next incarnation so on. Whichever it may be, coming into effect is must. For this, the Doer would be held in any circumstances."

"What would be the result of the Deed ?"

"When the Deed is done, something can be come about. This coming about may be constructive or destructive; useful or harmful and invitable or uninvitable. Whatever it may be the Doer is held for partaking of coming about or the result."

"What would be the development of the Deed ?"

"When the Deed is done, something can be brought into a state in which that something would be active or visible. Whichever development it may be the Doer is held to share in."

"What would be the sequel of the Deed ?"

"When the Deed is done, something in some other form would follow the something or something in some other form would be arisen out of same something. So, the Doer is held for that following or arising out."

"What would be the upshot of the Deed ?"

"When the Deed is done, something can be ultimately occurred. This occurance could be advantageous or disadvantageous. Whatever this occurance may be, the Doer would be held for the upshot."

Chapter-50

For any each and every 'I' whoever may be i.e. either The Believer-in 'I' or The Player-'I', would it be possible while keeping on without doing any ?"

"Not at all possible even for The Only "I"."

"I still remember and never forget which You told that The Only "I" don't do anything. Didn't You ?"

"Yes. I did. But You have forgotten that the undoing of The Only "I" would be too doing."

"When each and every 'I' would be The Only "I", why couldn't the undoing of each and every 'I', be too doing ?"

"The Only "I" do 'Will' only that too not for The Only "I"."

"Doesn't The Doing 'Will' of The Only "I" have Intention lies behind, Expectation from the Doing and scope for Aspiration to be arisen out from the Doing ?"

"The best question at first You have put in our dialoguing. Doesn't have the Intention, the Expectation and the Aspiration. The Only "I" do 'Will' for those each and every 'I' who were kept under cessation too not to attending their predetermined Deeds for a period which is honoured as the period of 'Not To Be Many' that equals in longness of the period of 'To Be Many'. When The Only "I" do 'Will' to be Many, some other each and every 'I' can also cherish Illusion that they would be separated from The Only "I" or they would not be The Only "I". For both sorts of each and every 'I', The Only "I" do 'Will' to be Many but not for The Only "I". Hence no Intention of The Only "I" would be there. The Only "I" would never expect anything from any each and every 'I', though, The Only "I" would be every each and every 'I' who had cherished the Illusion. Even The Only "I" would never expect that by dint of the 'Will' done, at least few or one might Regain the Unlost. Hence, no Expectation of The Only "I" would be there. Even The Only "I" would never aspire that all, many, few or at least one of all each and every 'I' must utilize the opportunity properly in the form of 'Will' done to be Many to know and learn what had been each and every 'I', what was and what would actually be eventually, for that, what each and every 'I' do to Regain the Unlost. Hence, no Aspiration of The Only "I" would be there."

Chapter-51

"Could any one of all each and every 'I' do or attend the Deed without having any Intention ?"

"Not only any one of all each and every 'I' but every one of all each and every 'I' also could do or attend the Deed without having any Intention."

"How ?"

"The Player-'I' must opt or select The Believer-in 'I' to worship that Believer-in 'I' without intending to indulge either in carnal desires or wordly comforts that can be received or offered by The Believer-in 'I'. Whatever comforts received, The Player-'I' must resubmit the same comforts to The Believer-in 'I' only and keep renunciation of the comfortableness with The Player-'I'. If The Player-'I' feel that The Player-'I' enjoy the comfortableness, it would be that enjoying which would be available in 'The Many' which exists for a long only. So, The Player-'I', who enjoy this comfortableness, would deserve to be gone on only in 'The Many' which follows forthcoming 'Not To Be Many'. In the course of worshipping The Believer-in 'I', The Player-'I', whenever, do participate in physical intercourse, The Player-'I' must not take pleasure in carnal desires granted for The Bliss in which state one would be deprived of all kinds of afflictions. Because The Bliss is the third character of The Only "I" even of each and every 'I' as each and every 'I' am also The Only "I". The physical body of The Player-'I' or The Believer-in 'I' is the physical property only made of five basic or fundamental elements. The First and foremost purpose of physical intercourse taken place by The Believer-in 'I' and The Player-'I' is to prepare a physical body for another each and every 'I' to be entered to resume The Practice to regain the Unlost which was paused in previous incarnation whenever each and every 'I' would be brought out by means of prepared physical body. So, the Purpose of physical intercourse of The Believer-in 'I' and The Player-'I' is not to reach the state of The Bliss which couldn't be possible by the physical intercourse. When The Believer-in 'I' and The Player-'I' enjoy the physical intercourse, then, they would cherish the Illusion that they would be enjoying or experiencing the Bliss in lieu of the orgasm. Hence, The Player-'I' must not be eager for physical intercourse only with The Believer-in 'I' whom The Player-'I' do worship."

"Must not The Player-'I' enjoy the physical intercourse with The Believer-in 'I' whom The Player-'I' worship ?"

"The Player-'I' must enjoy the physical intercourse with The Believer-in 'I' whom The Player-'I' worship as much as possible to The Player-'I'."

"How can it be possible when The Player-'I' must not be eager for physical intercourse ?"

"When The Player-'I' would be eager for physical intercourse with The Believer-in 'I' whom The Player-'I' worship, then, the carnal Desire could get the upper hand of the Mind which straightforward behaviour towards the Practice meant to regain the Unlost. Resulting in, The Practice must be affected. The Mind is so which has to be applied by the Intellect. When The Player-'I' would be eager for the physical intercourse only with The Believer-in 'I' whom The Player-'I' do worship, then, the worshipping can be replaced by the desiring. If there is the Desire only, then, the worshipping would not be necessary. In the absence of worshipping The Believer-in 'I', The Player-'I' could not be able to minimize Doingness. Minimizing Doingness means to be reaching to get rid of cherishing The Illusion. In the absence of worshipping The Believer-in 'I', The Player-'I' would yield to the Temptation of the Carnal Desire and can enjoy the physical intercourse with The Believer-in 'I' who am not same The Believer-in 'I' whom this Player-'I' do worship. Then the Practice, which could be observed by only Homo sapien being, would be comprehensively annihilated. So, The Player-'I' must worship only one Believer-in 'I' and enjoy physical intercourse with this Believer-in 'I' only as a part of worshipping. If The Player-'I' does so accordingly that Player-'I' can do so as much possible as that Player-'I' do. When The Player-'I' could be able to be free from the lasciviousness immediate after consummation of physical intercourse and keep not to be under impact of that intercourse until particularized or specifies occasion is occurred."

"Who could particularize or specify certain occasion ?"

"None other else. Both The Player-'I' and The Believer-in 'I' ought to particularize or specify. They could only do so for themselves."

"How could they do so ? which would be the parameter that defines the particularized specified occasion ?"

"Their Practice meant to regain the Unlost would regulate their instinct. Hence their Instinct would let themselves know at what occasion they have to partake in physical intercourse. Learning the letting them know the regulated Instinct would be the parameter."

"Could both be let to know so simultaneously ?"

"Yes. Both could be done accordingly."

Chapter-52

"For them, what would be the Physical intercourse ?"

"As Homo sapien beings, at first, both don't let any others watch their physical intercourse either openly or secretly."

"Why don't they let ?"

"Not only for them but also for all Homo sapien beings, physical intercourse would be a part of worshipping. Homo sapien beings are not Voluptuous beings which couldn't be restricted to copulate secretly."

"How would physical intercourse be a part of worshipping for Homo sapien beings ?"

"Any being, in course of assuming incarnations from a sort of being to another of being, if deserves to assume incarnation of human being to do Practice to regain what is Unlost and enters accordingly into the body of a Homo sapien, must observe the Practice without any interruption or having been marred. The Physical intercourse of Homo sapien beings must lead them to be immersed in the Mental Intercourse. For that immersion only, as Ritualistic beings, The Believer-in 'I' and The Player-'I' must observe their Physical Intercourse as a part of worshipping."

"Why couldn't Voluptuous beings be restricted to copulate secretly ?"

"Voluptuous beings don't have the Intellect which could decide what has to be done and not to be done."

"Why musn't The Player-'I' and The Believer-in 'I' be let any other Homo sapien beings even secretly to watch their physical intercourse ?"

"No assurance could be given by even any Ritualistic being, who has reached the upright highest stage in the Practice, that certain Homo sapien being is absolutely free from Voluptuousness. Hence, the quite full scope would be there for that watched physical intercourse be made widely known."

"What will happen, if it is made widely known ?"

"That, which has been in the know and will have been made known, would ever be The Only "I" who would be beyond 'The Many'. So, That, which hasn't been kept as 'in the know', is made widely known, couldn't be kept as 'in the know'. Hence, the participants in physical intercourse couldn't reach stage in which they ought to be as 'in the know'."

"When that secretly watched physical intercourse is made widely known by those who watch it secretly, why should the participants of that physical intercourse be punished accordingly ?"

"Because, they are Homo sapien beings who are ever expected to become Ritualistic beings."

"Then, why shouldn't those, who watch secretly, be punished ?"

"Those, who watch secretly, must be sentenced with rigorous punishment."

"Rigorous punishment ! What is that ?"

"Those Homo sapien beings, who watch physical intercourse of a couple of Homo sapien beings while having the physical intercourse as a part of worshipping, couldn't assume incarnation of Homo sapien being in any forthcoming generations until 'The Many' lasts."

"Oh ! It would be the Most terrible and horrible and the Most horrible and terrible. If some Homo sapien being or beings do so, wouldn't any confession be there to be made by that or those ?"

"No, any kind of confession would not be there."

"Then, why has the concept, 'confession' been brought about ?"

"The concept, confession has been brought out not to be made and heard whenever the worshipping being done in course of observing the Practice marred. If any Homo sapien being is disturbed or interrupted in individual items of job or work which isn't exclusively pertaining to worshipping or the Practice, then only, that Homo sapien being who commits so is allowed or permitted to make confession."

"Who could be able to hear so ?"

"None other else. At first that Homo sapien being who is disturbed or interrupted. Second is that Homo sapien being who has committed when it can be able to discern it and it'self'. At last the Third is that Homo sapien being who has reached the stage of Ritualistic being which could envision The Only "I" who would only be The Only "I", each and every 'I' and 'The Many' too. The Only "I" as The Only "I" would be beyond all of each and every 'I' and 'The Many'."

"Could so, who do hear, and pardon ?"

"Other than the Disturbed or the Interrupted being, the being who commits and the Ritualistic, no any other Homo sapien being would or could pardon."

Chapter-53

"What would be the occasion for that both to have physical intercourse as a part of their worshipping ?"

"Any couple of The Player-'I' and The Believer-in 'I' would be permitted or allowed to have physical intercourse during the sixth three hours period of a day which day would be reckoned from the sunrise to the next sunrise."

"Wouldn't any other three hours period other than the sixth be allowed or permitted ?"

"Never. Never be done."

"Why would that sixth period only be done ?"

"Yes, during the sixth three hours period of the day all Homo sapien beings must get to sleep. They are ever advised and wished to go to sleep. i.e. deep or sound sleep during the seventh three hours period of the day and asked to wake up in the eighth three hours period. All Homo sapien beings ought to complete all their morning ablutions during the eighth three hours period. They are sternly commanded to complete all kinds of their deeds by fifth three hours period of day at any cost. Even no deed is ever allowed or permitted to be attended or done during the last. i.e. seventh three hours period of day."

"Why are Homo sapien beings only commanded to observe such occasion ?"

"Because, they are not Voluptuous beings which are meant

to respond their 'sense' without applying their Mind which doesn't have Intellect which could decide to do or not to do."

"What would happen, if Homo sapien beings do have physical intercourse during any three hours period of their choice other than sixth period ?"

"Physical Intercourse being had between a male Homo sapien being and a female Homo sapien, if is viewed by other Homo sapien beings whoever may be, must cause that viewers to be debauched or seduced or deflowered."

"What would such viewers do if they are caused to be debauched ?"

"Those viewers, who are caused to be debauched, would lose the theological virtues which preserve goodness and excellence of Homo sapien beings to go on as pure human beings free from maximum Voluptuousness by dint of which without applying their Intellect they can baffle those Homo sapien beings who are observing their Practice honestly."

"What would such viewers do if they are caused to be seduced ?"

"Those viewers, who are caused to be seduced, would be tempted themselves and would tempt others to commit sin."

"Commit sin ! What is the Sin ?"

"The Sin is that which causes viewers to violate their own propriety and let those whom they commit do same themselves."

"So, The Sin would never be excusable or forgivable or pardonable and condoned too. Would it be ?"

"Yes. You have precisely divulged. In Truth, Sin is more than all crimes, offences and felons etc. It couldn't be defined with only worldly mindedness."

"Why couldn't it be done accordingly ?"

"I have obviously told that it couldn't be defined. But I can let You to know what is the Sin in poetic manner.

Know not You or She or He or all of You,
You, She, He and 'I' not are others from 'I'.

'I' ever do one, few, many for the sake of 'I'
As apart from or beyond 'I', none would be there.

Know not You or She or He ever does like 'I'
But not for the sake of 'I' whom am as 'Self' of
You or She or He but not any other, nobody would be there.

The Doing, which is not for the sake of 'I' or 'Self'
Is only the Sin that 'Self' of You or She or He couldn't ever
Either excuse or forgive or pardon or condone."

"You mean even a Homo sapien being, whoever it may be, if commits the Sin, wouldn't either excuse or forgive or pardon or condone itself too ! Don't You ?"

"Yes. I mean so what You have just learnt."

"What would such viewers do if they are caused to be deflowered ?"

"Having been deflowered means having been deprived of virginity. In the course of worshipping The Believer-in 'I', The Player-'I' would be authorized to submit Virginity of The Player-'I' while having physical intercourse. Submitting Virginity ever stands for submitting her'Self' to his'self' as The Believer-in 'I' am a

Man is he who ever endeavours
To envision his'Self' as the 'Self'.
He does every deed for the 'Self' only.
He ever stands for the 'Cause' only.
He would lead his life as the life only
But not as of his own life.
In this life, one couldn't be
Any other but only the 'I'.
The Player 'I' am a
Woman is she who ever endeavours
To be merged into this 'Life' only."

"You mean no separate life of his own and no separate life of her own are commanded, Don't You ?"

"Exactly You have got the point. The Life of The Player-'I' and The Believer-in 'I' would be there."

"If a female Homo sapien being is lost her virginity with a male Homo sapien being whom that female Homo sapien being doesn't worship or like this male Homo sapien being, can then also, her virginity be treated as deflowered ?"

"Physically it can be treated accordingly, if that female Homo sapien being doesn't enjoy in good faith that deflowering virginity."

"Can another Believer-in 'I' other than that male Homo sapien being accept that female Homo sapien being whose virginity is deflowered ?"

"When The Believer-in 'I' can learn that in good faith that female Homo sapien being hasn't enjoyed her deflowering virginity and do worship This Believer-in 'I' sincerely and honestly, then, The Believer-in 'I' can do."

"Can deflowering virginity be acceptable ?"

"Never."

"Then.. ?"

"Now, we are discussing Virginity which has been lost without having the infatuation and the mainspring on part of that female Homo sapien being whose virginity is lost. Virginity isn't the matter pertaining to Macro body only but also to Micro body too. As far as concerned to hymen, it is the matter pertaining to Macro body. When Virginity is being lost of that losing virginity is enjoyed for the least span of second, then that matter must be pertaining to Micro body. Whenever the Micro body is either effected or affected, then, that each and every 'I' who am is that female Homo sapien being couldn't be free from the S'i'n. If not enjoyed and effected or affected, then, it might be accepted. If accordingly accepted, that female Homo sapien being can get deservedness to worship sincerely and devotedly while ignoring the entire inferior complexion put. The problem would be with The Believer-in 'I' who have to trust that female Homo sapien being who has lost virginity without having the infatuation and the mainspring on part of that female Homo sapien being."

"What would be the 'S'i'n' ? Is it separate from 's'i'n' ?"

"Same sin. But I have used word, sin as 'S'i'n wittily. Because when either a male Homo sapien being or a female Homo sapien being succumbs to 'senses', then, 'i' who stand for each and every 'I' would be fettered in 'Nemesis' to get rid of which is only The Regaining the Unlost. So, sin can be supposed as acronym of words of senses, i(each and every 'I') and Nemesis. Hence, S'i'n is the acronym which isn't separated from 'sin'."

"But You have not answered exactly yet to my question that what such deflowered viewers do. Have You ?"

"Those deflowered viewers who enjoy losing their virginity can neglect and ignore all theological virtues set by Those Ritualistic beings who could have envisioned The Only "I" who would be only Everything, Everyone, even Nothing or Zero. They could have also envisioned that all which could be cherished as 'Many' than 'Solo' or 'One' would be too The Only "I". By virtue of observing these Theological Virtues, The Player-'I' and The Believer-in 'I' could do The Practice without being fluctuated until they reach the Ultimate End. Owing to negligent and ignorant behaviour of these viewers towards The Player-'I' and The Believer-in 'I', the Practice meant to Regaining the Unlost of these Player-'I' and Believer-in 'I' could get fluctuated."

"How would their behaviour be ?"

"In both, physically i.e. bodily and Mentally i.e. in speech. By means of their body language i.e. their gestures and movements that are used to express their thoughts and feelings, they can or could infatuate The Player-'I' or The Believer-in 'I' or both. Their body language along with their speech can or could fascinate The Player-'I' and captivate The Believer-in 'I'. Resulting in, The Practice of The Player-'I' or The Believer-in 'I' could be fluctuated. One's fluctuated practice could fluctuate Another one's too. Besides, those Homo sapien beings, who haven't yet known and learnt themselves that they have to become or flourish to be The Player-'I' and The Believer-in 'I' to do Practice meant to Regain the Unlost are under impact of cherishing the Illusion that among them each and every 'I' would not be separated from one another and among them each and every 'I' would not be The Only "I"."

"How can The Player 'I' and The Believer –in 'I' protect or defend themselves from this behaviour ?"

"Both The Player-'I' and The Believer-in 'I' must ever be alert while keeping themselves away from this behaviour of such Homo sapien being as a part of their Practice and

They must know that humanness is different
From beastliness in which 'state' a being
Reacts as a slave to its own bodily senses;
Humanness is that in which 'state' a being
Could control its senses as their Master;
A human being shouldn't hear what its senses tell
But listen to what its 'Self' say;

Hence, all Homo sapien beings i.e. human beings especially who could be doing The Practice meant to Regain what actually they have Unlost must know, learn and accept that though each and every 'I' would be in all living beings, human beings are different from other beings."

Chapter-54

"What about other beings in whom, as You have just told, there would be each and every 'I', if they watch or view the physical intercourse is being had between The Player-'I' and The Believer-in 'I' ?"

"The Player-'I' and The Believer-in 'I' must not let any being or beings too other than Homo sapien beings watch or view their physical intercourse being had."

"Are they too caused to be seduced, debauched and deflowered ?"

"They couldn't know and learn what would be seduction, debauching and deflowering."

"Then, what would be wrong with The Player-'I' and The Believer-in 'I', if both let other beings than Homo sapien beings watch or view ?"

"Each and every living being does have the Mind which could get responded though that Mind could not have Intellect to apply or decide. Getting responded would also be a doing done by the Mind only. You have been already told that each and every doing must have been comprised of the Deed, the Mind and the Speech. Hence, it is crystal clear that The Player-'I' and The Believer-in 'I', who have let the beings other than Homo sapien beings watch or view their own physical intercourse being had, would be held for the Mind of those beings be attracted or corrupted in form of getting responded."

"Do they react whenever they get responded accordingly ?"

"They may not react physically. But their Mind must be affected in some extension. Hence, their Voluptuousness can be enhanced."

"Do they get themselves their enhanced Voluptuousness subsided ?"

"Not possible for them as they are not doers of the Deed. They act and react according to functioning of their senses."

"Then, owing to their enhanced Voluptuousness what will happen ?"

"In Truth, The Voluptuousness would be one of entities such as time and space. As long as The Many (the creation) exists, the Voluptuousness subsists among the beings including Human beings. So, if Voluptuousness is enhanced, all Human beings including Ritualistic beings might also be affected. Therefore, The Player-'I' and The Believer-in 'I' who causes for this enhancement of Voluptuousness would be held."

Chapter-55

"If The Player-'I' and The Believer-in 'I' have their physical intercourse while not letting any other either Homo sapien beings or Voluptuous beings by observing the occasion, can they get enabled to have Mental Intercourse ?"

"Earlier on, they can be awarded the best couple which have achieved the steadiness along with decency and dignity which couldn't be abated or diminished even destroyed. In course of observing this occasion, both gradually arrive at the stage of steadfastness."

"What would be the Award ?"

"Actually The Award would be the Birth."

"How ?"

"Each and every birth as a Homo sapien being would be The Award. The birth as a Homo sapien being is the most advantageous to each and every 'I'. Because,

FOR ANY EACH 'I' FROM ANY SORT
THE BEST BODY IS OF HUMAN ONLY.

The human being could only think over
To retain its humanity
While getting ready to do something.
It could imagine consequences,
Then suppose to do or not.
It could view reduction to come
And envision ultimate happening

As per its visions it could decide
And abide by its 'Self-decision'."

"When The Birth as a Homo sapien is the most advantageous as You told, why isn't the Homo sapien being as a human being efficacious in many cases ?"

"Because, though each and every 'I' who would enter body of Homo sapien and have all things, anyone or few of such things are only ever noted. This each and every 'I' first of all know and learn which things are those. This knowing and learning is honoured as 'Self-knowing'. If this human being itself devotes this self-knowing and do Practice by dint of this self-knowing, then, it could be efficacious. To be efficacious would be The Award which has been, in Truth, conferred on this each and every 'I' by this each and every 'I'."

"How could this each and every 'I' confer The Award on this each and every 'I' ?"

"Because, each and every 'I' would be only The Only "I". So, this each and every 'I' as 'Self-knower' each and every 'I' could confer The Award on this i.e. Self- Knower each and every 'I'. No other each and every 'I' than this each and every 'I' would do so, though, other each and every 'I' could do so."

"You mean The Player-'I' could only do such Practice which causes to confer on The Deserved Award on The Player-'I'. At the same time The Believer-in 'I' could only do such Practice which causes to confer on The Deserved Award on The Believer-in 'I'. Don't You ?"

"There, You are."

"If The Player-'I' and The Believer-in 'I' devote other things, separately, then....?"

"Devoting other things such as occupation, administration, Art etc. couldn't affect The worshipping of The Player-'I' and The gracing of The Believer-in 'I'. Because 'Devoting' would enable The Player-'I' to worship The Believer-in 'I' more attentively and The Believer-in 'I' to grace The Player-'I' more affectionately."

"So, That Player 'I' who worship The Believer-in 'I' more attentively and That Believer-in 'I' who grace The Player-'I' more affectionately would be conferred The Award of The Best couple on. Then Achieving the steadiness means what ? For which is steadiness required ?"

"The steadiness means to be balanced, to be regular in movement, to be regular in behaviour and habits and to be constant. The couple which has achieved this steadiness must hold it evermore."

"Why must this couple do so evermore ?"

"If both The Player-'I' and The Believer-in 'I' or any one of both is debilitated for the least span of time within no second that would fall from the achieved stature to the most inferior level. This can be treated as 'The Fall of The Being.' Actually there wouldn't be 'Fall' of any being from anywhere. So, jointly both The Player-'I' and The Believer-in 'I' must hold steadiness in all their movements and behaviour etc. If they fall from their achieved stature, They are to once again commence their Practice from the ABC."

"What would be the steadfastness ?"

"When the steadiness is being held persistently, this steadiness would be gradually metamorphed into the steadifastness. The couple, which arrives the stage of steadifastness, could never be affected and corrupted by any means. Besides, This Player-'I' and This Believer-in 'I' would never be confused or bewildered or embarrassed."

Chapter-56

"When both The Player-'I' and The Believer-in 'I' arrive at the stage of steadfastness, what would be remained for both to do ?"

"The stage of steadfastness would be the beginning of the Mental Intercourse which could be had without having physical intercourse. The Mental Intercourse even doesn't need Love Making also. So, The Player-'I' and The Believer-in 'I' do have Mental Intercourse without touching physical bodies of each other. They even need not to see, look at, watch and view each other at any time. They also need not to hear and listen to each other at all times. But The Player-'I' could accurately tell how The Believer-in 'I' would be viewing her and The Believer-in 'I' could exactly listen to what The Player-'I' would be chanting in course of worshipping The Believer-in 'I'. All, these looking at, watching, viewing, hearing and listening would be, without affecting the sensual organs, done by The Mind i.e. the first inward sense. So, no physical appetite for having intercourse could be found in that Mental Intercourse. As long as sensual organs are not affected, the Doing couldn't be taken Doingness granted for. Hence, Doingness would be merged into The Beingness, Therefore there would be nothing remained for the Both to do."

"When there would be remained nothing to be done, why couldn't Doing be taken Doingness granted for ?"

"Because, still There would be two i.e. The Player-'I' and The Believer-in 'I' seemed in Existence."

"Seemed in Existence !?"

"Yes. Every 'He' i.e. The Believer-in 'I' and every 'She' i.e. The Player-'I' who are doing the Practice do seem in Existence."

"Don't Both be in Existence ?"

"No, In Truth, They wouldn't be."

"How ?"

"I narrate this item in poetic matter. Listen.

He is 'He' who is 'H'aving 'E'xistence
From time immemorial to forever
Neither takes birth nor dies ever.

Get dressed and undressed He does.
He acts as dressed but not as He does be.
Despite Act isn't of Him, He does of 'his'.

She 'S'eems 'H'aving 'E'xistence separately.
But separation never be found in 'she'.
In dressing, doing and taking she is too same.

The acting looks differed from The Act.
The 'ing' only puts full stop to The Act.
Then 'H'aving in both merges into the
Existence."

"You mean 'HE' stands for The Only "I" in true. 'SHE' stands for The Believer-in 'I' and The Player-'I'. Don't You ?"

"Exactly. I appreciate You. You have got the point quite correctly."

"When would this seemed-existence get elasped absolutely ?"

"In the course of Mental Intercourse being had by them, they use to get bit by bit, drop by drop, little by little, piece by piece, step by step rid of cherishing the Illusion that both The Player-'I' and The Believer-in 'I' would not be separate from each other."

"Bit by bit means…?"

"Bit by bit The Player-'I' could know and learn that the body in which The Player-'I' would be each and every 'I'."

"Drop by drop means…?"

"Drop by drop The Player-'I' could know and learn that in both of The Player-'I' and The Believer-in 'I' and in all bodies of Homo sapien beings and Voluptuous beings, there would be same each and every 'I'."

"Little by little means…?"

"Little by little The Player-'I' and The Believer-in 'I' know and learn that in Beingness and Doingness both have been differed from each other though would be one and the same in true."

"Piece by piece means…?"

"Piece by piece both The Player-'I' and The Believer-in 'I' must merge of their each Doingness in the Beingness which would be one and the same in each but would be as two in each."

"Step by step by means..?"

"Step by step both The Player-'I' and The Believer-in 'I' would know and learn that They would be The 'Be' without having Doingness."

Chapter-57

"Would the Doingness of The Believer-in 'I' be same which would be of The Player-'I' ?"

"The Doingness would be one and the same of The Player-'I' and The Believer-in 'I'. But the doing of The Player-'I' differs from that of The Believer-in 'I'."

"What kind of doing would be of The Player-'I' ?"

"As long as The Player-'I' do desire to have her own identity, individuality, entity, standing for her own life, standing for own cause and supposing her responsibility, The Player-'I' would have her own doing. When The Player-'I' know, learn and Stand for The identity, individuality, entity and standing for the 'Life' of The Believer-in 'I' and standing for the cause of The Believer-in 'I', since then, the 'doing' of The Player-'I' would merge into the Beingness of both The Player-'I' and The Believer-in 'I' as The 'Do' would be in 'Many' forms but The 'Be' would be only One. When doing of The Player-'I' is merged into the Beingness, then, The Player-'I' would be as

She doesn't have any likes and dislikes
Other than He (The Believer-in 'I') does.
She doesn't have her own words also.
She is not only a follower to Him
But the best companion too at every time.
She never doubts and suspects Him.
She never supposes to challenge Him.
She is ever faithful and trustful to Him.
She serves Him for her 'Self'.
And receives His grace for His'Self'."

"What kind of doing would be of The Believer-in 'I' ?"

"The Believer-in 'I' must know and learn that every each and every 'I' do contain the Art which would be the collection of skill, practice and knowledge."

"When The Believer-in 'I' must know and learn 'skill', what should The Believer-in 'I' do ?"

"The Believer-in 'I' should learn the 'Skill' to draw the exact meaning of and every word of any language which The Believer-in 'I' come to light. The Language is a means to express the idea occurred and communicate occurred idea. Without skill, communication can't be done in proper. When the occurred idea is expressed and communicated effectively, then, each and every 'I' who express and communicate to another each and every 'I' would be educated for the subject at last. This learning the 'Skill' could be possible to each and every 'I' who believe in 'I' i.e. The Player-'I' too."

"Shouldn't The Player-'I' know and learn This Skill ?"

"Why shouldn't. When The Player-'I' learn This Skill, The Player-'I' will believe in 'I' who am each and every 'I', The Believer-in 'I' and The Only "I". As a more doer than The Believer-in 'I', it would be better for The Player-'I' to worship The Believer-in 'I'. Because, to believe-in 'I' could be possible when the believer could be one who could envision internally. As a more doer than The Believer-in 'I', for The Player-'I' to be so would be hardly possible."

"When The Believer-in 'I' know and learn 'Practice', what should The Believer-in 'I' do ?"

"The Believer-in 'I' must know and learn 'Practice' that Doing which has been learnt to be done. When this Doing is to be done repeatedly, this repetition of doing is the 'Practice'."

"Would Practice, which is frequently being told during our dialoguing as The Practice meant to Regaining the Unlost, be same Practice ?"

"No, this practice would not be so. Though each and every 'I' would be The Only "I" who wouldn't need repetition to do 'will', no each and every 'I' could not learn anything in a single-attempt. To learn something by heart or without misgiving, that each and every 'I' have to do so repeatedly. The things being learned by this practice enable The Believer-in 'I' to believe-in The Only "I" who would be told as The 'Thing' or The 'One' who would only be in The Existence from beginningless to endlessness. To hold observing the believing in The Only "I" would only be The Practice of The Believer-in 'I' meant to Regain the Unlost. The same or some other things being learned by this practice enable The Player-'I' to worship The Believer-in 'I' as The Only "I". This worshipping The Believer-in 'I' would only be The Practice to The Player-'I' meant to Regain the Unlost."

"When The Believer-in 'I' must acquire the knowledge what should The Believer-in 'I' do ?"

"Here, knowledge means 'to be aware' of needed-items for some things to be done. By acquiring such knowledge The Believer-in 'I' can know and learn how to do anything skillfully while keeping alertness to be beyond doubt until the task accomplished. When The Believer-in 'I' arrive at stage, then, That Believer-in 'I' could be He who would be without exception as HE'art'."

"HE'art' ! ? What would HE'art' stand for ?"

"I can narrate HE'art' in poetic manner. Listen !

He contains Art
Which isn't something
Separate from Him.

He is expressed
As some distinguishably
Ever from Him.

He is seen
As some other
Different from Him.

He is understood
As another thing.
Dissimilar to Him.

He is envisioned
As 'He' when
'Art' emerges from Him."

"What is difference between He and 'He' ?"

"He is The Believer-in 'I' whom The Player-'I' would not yet opted and selected to worship whereas 'He' is The Believer-in 'I' whom The Player-'I' worshipped and merged Her'Self' into His'Self', thus remained as "S'HE'"."

Chapter-58

" "S'HE"'! who would be "S'HE"'?

"Except The Only "I", You have already been told, Nothing or None would be there. So, "S'HE"' would be The Only "I"."

"I still remember that what would be told either as 'One' or as 'Thing' would be The Only "I". "I" that too without preceded by 'The' and 'Only'. I even remember that "I" wouldn't too address "I" as "I" though "I" could address "I" as "I". Therefore, who would be "S'HE"' other than "I" when The Player –'I' merge into The Believer-in 'I' ?"

"Regarding 'The', it could be understood 'The' is an article which precedes a Noun which is in question. Regarding 'Only', I narrate it in poetic manner. Listen.

'Only' "I" do 'Will'.
"I" mean except "I"
No other is there.

"I" only do 'Will'
"I" mean along with "I"
Others are there.

Those others are
From 'Will' which isn't
Other than 'Only' "I".

"I" do only 'Will' '
'I" mean "I" amn't the doer
Like others who do 'Many'.

Those doers of 'Many'
Envisage themselves ever
As They aren't "I" but 'I'.

"I" do 'Will' 'Only'.
"I" mean "I" don't do any others
Which doings are from 'Will'.

'Only' qualifies "I" and 'Will'.
But 'Will' is done for all others.
Who couldn't do 'Will' ever.

So, 'Only' does qualifies."

"Who do "I" mean ?"

"To draw meaning to "I" couldn't be possible to You and I even any each and every 'I'. I am sure Even "I" might not give accurate or exact answer. So, I narrate this item too in poetic manner. Listen.

What would be the meaning of "I" ?
Who could draw and give that to any ?
Among those, who could draw and give,
"I" would be too as "I" would be sure
That "I" would never do so and so though
"I" would be ever Omniscient and Omnipotent.

It would never be the reason to draw and give
That "I" would be the single word even single
Lettered which represents each and every One
Even each and every thing when personified.

When as the word, "I" represent One that word
Must stand for that One only for another
One who looks in equal with One in the same
Way as the word, "I" represent only that thing
Which is personified but not another thing.
So, "I" suppose no problem is there as the
Word, "I" would, at all times, be crystal clear.

Each and every One, who addresses Oneself,
Does as "I" but addressed "I" wouldn't ever be
Actually that one but that one can be only so
Who have been in the State in which that One
Would be the some which One takes as ever
Separated from the All without learning the All.

Though One knows and Learns as Another One
Than One too addresses Oneself as "I" only,
Earlier One always addresses Another One as
You, He, She, or It, so does It, She, He or You.
Hence, once again it is crystal clear that each
And every one could never be sure that who,
Among One, You, He, She or It would be "I" ?

Even "I" who do 'WILL' to be 'Many' for a long
And not to be 'Many' for same long wouldn't
Endorse whether the meaning of "I" would be
The 'WILL' due to which "I" would be only 'each
And every one' because None and No Thing
Could never be beyond "I" but "I" would be so.
Being beyond the All which can be looked as
Uncountable and the All which can be done as
Separated from one another, "I" would be the
All and the All without being as both the All.
So, "I" would be either the All and the All or

"I" would be only "I" also "I" would be neither
The All and the All nor "I" would be only "I"
But "I" would be only "I" as well as both the All.

Thus, "I" could explain What am "I", How am "I"
And what "I" do but "I" too could not define "I"
Or draw and give proper and suitable meaning
To "I" when "I" put a query, 'What do "I" mean' ?"

"Would "S'HE"' be "I" ? You have to yet to answer. Don't You ?"

"Yes. I have to. I have not completed my answer. To This too I narrate in poetic manner. Listen.

"S'HE"' would be 'She'
Who could bring out
'HE' from "S'HE"' to
Bring up 'HE' to be
"S'HE"', ultimately.

At first, "S'HE"' might
Have been as she only,
Subsequently she must
Prove herself in all in all
Thus, she could establish
'She' who dedicates to he
To turn He to 'He' to be "S'HE"'.

"S'HE"' would only be visioned
But nor "SHE" who in true
Observes penance not to be
"SHE" ever but to reach as
Only "HE" who could only
Be envisioned as "I" who

Have been going on as "I"
Before the Past to Beyond
The Future which both have
Neither Beginning nor Ending."

"After merging The Player-'I' into The Believer-in 'I', there would be scope for them to obsess that both would be now One not two. So,"S'HE"'."

"Would this obsessing be the cherishing of the Illusion ?"

"Never. Because both The Player-'I' and The Believer-in 'I' would now obsess that both they would be One without having separation between them. So, this obsessing wouldn't be The cherishing of Illusion."

"But You have told that they would be One. When They would be One and not Two, how could it be obsessing ?"

"They would obsess that they would be One now. So, 'Now' indicates Time which wouldn't be The Truth, The Untruth, The Untruly Truth and The truly Untruth."

"Yes. I remember. What would be wrong with that as Time, if 'Now' could be perceptible ?"

"First of all, You ever keep on your Mind that which or what could be perceptible to the bodily senses or the Mind, that wouldn't be The Truth."

"So, wouldn't "S'HE"' be The Truth as The Only "I" ?

"Even "S'HE'" wouldn't be The Untruth like the 'Will' of The Only "I" as 'To be Many' and 'Not to be Many'."

"When "S'HE'" wouldn't be Truth or Untruth why should The Player-'I' and The Believer-in 'I' have done The Practice to be The Truth i.e. Regained The Unlost ?"

"They have done the Practice but have not regained what they Unlost ?"

"To be "S'HE'" not Regaining the Unlost ?"

"No doubt. They have Regaining 'One' but not 'None'."

"What! What would be One and what would be None ?"

"One would mean there would be One and no another one would not be there than One. None would mean That One would too not be there."

"Would that None be Zero ?"

"There You are."

"What would be Zero ?"

"'Zero' would be forever "I".

"I" would be forevermore 'Zero'"

Which could be honoured as Nothing
Which could never be treated as Thing
Which could be understood as Matter
Which could be taken granted for Subject

Which could be studied as Topic
Which could be discussed as Theme
Which could be brought together as Question
Which could be arisen as Problem
Which could be dealt as Solution
Which could be illustrated as Salvation
Which could be withstood as 'Zero'.

So, if You couldn't answer to a question or no answer could be with You for any, that would be 'Zero'."

"How ?"

"What would You have understood about The Only "I" ?"

"The Only "I" would be Omni-Present."

"Present means what ?"

"Either Place or Space."

"If so, there would have been Place or Space for The Only "I" to be pervaded. But The Only "I" would never pervade from here to there or there to here through Place or Space."

"Then, Where would The Only "I" be ?"

"You suppose what and which pervades would be The Only "I"."

"Through which or what The Only "I" do pervade ?"

" 'Which' or 'What' would not be there for The Only "I" to pervade through."

"Without having any means to be pervaded through, would The Only "I" do pervade ?"

"No, The Only "I" would not pervade. But The Only "I" would be there."

"Where would The Only "I" be there ?"

"Everywhere The Only "I" would be."

"What does Everywhere mean or refer to ?"

"Everywhere does mean The Only "I" and Everywhere does refer to The Only "I"."

"How ?"

"Because, There would be The Only "I" only. Other than The Only "I", either any thing or things or any one or some would not be there outside The Only "I" or beyond The Only "I"."

"Have The Only "I" the Outside ?"

"No, Not possible. If You imagine that You would start a journey from a point in The Only "I", then, You could go any long at anyside. But You couldn't find border of The Only "I" as The Only "I" would be borderless. Hence, no Outside of The Only "I" would be there as anything or anyone Which or who is supposed, at present, as in existence.would ever be in The Only "I" but couldn't be in Outside which wouldn't be anyside of The Only "I"."

"Does the word, 'Space' mean 'Zero' ?"

"Never. 'Space' would stand for the Place which would not be made of Matter but not Zero."

"Wouldn't 'Space' contain 'Sky' also which would be among five basic elements ?"

"No. sky would be too 'Space'."

"Wouldn't The Space and The Sky be one and the same ?"

"Would never be. But The Sky would be like The Space and The Space would be like The Sky. Alike there would be five spaces or skies. All these spaces or skies would never be The Only "I". when The Only "I" do 'Will' to be 'Many', all these skies and spaces exist in this 'Many'.When The Only "I" do 'Will' 'Not to be Many', they would merge in this 'Not to be Many'."

"All, which have been evaluated in our dialoguing, would be all right. But 'I' have not yet got cleared where "I" am ? Could You answer exactly ?"

"To answer where "I" am would not be possible. But in Poetic manner I can try to narrate. Listen!

"I" seem as "I" would be
From a point to another.

"I" am cherished as "I"
Would pervade between
This point to That point.

"I" am also done as "I"
Would do between Up
That couldn't be reached
And Down that couldn't be
Fathomed now or then.

"I" am even done as "I"
Would have a central
Point from which same
Length of radiuses get
Over circumference at all.

"I" am further done as "I"
Would permeate afterwards
The circumference at a distant
That couldn't be ever measured.
"I" am as well deduced as "I"
Could be at each and every
Point while "I" am pervading
Everywhere simultaneously.

But "I" would be "I" only as
"I" wouldn't have any points
At anywhere even no radii
Also no circumference that
Has afterwards and "I" am
Not a Thing which could be
At each and every point and
Pervade everywhere concurrently

As "I" am Nothing, in true, who
Would and could be Any and
Every as What "I" do 'Will' at
That "I" might even could be."

"So, "S'HE'" ought to Yet regain this Nothingness."

"There You are."

"Could "S'HE'" regain ?"

"As "S'HE'", "S'HE'" could get to be Nothing."

"When? During 'To be Many' only ?"

"Yes. If so happened."

"When The Only "I" do 'WILL' 'Not To Be Many', then, ?"

"Nothing would have been. Nothing would last as Nothing. Nothing would contain in no thing and no one. No time could pass or elapse. Nothing comprise of any. No letter would have been. No figure could have been. So would be Zero. Zero would have been Omniscient. All casual bodies who have lasted during 'To Be Many' would have been going on as casual bodies without having Micro bodies and Macro bodies but none of casual bodies would have separate existence of casual body. Entity of each and every casual body would have been as Nothing in Nothing or in Zero. So, Zero would have been Omniscient. Zero would have been Omnipotent. Though each and every casual body would have been Nothing in Nothing, Zero would have been with the cause of each and every casual body. But that cause would have no existence separately. Zero would have been Omnipresent. Sky, Space and Place would have been Nothing in Nothing. Beginning and ending would have been Nothing in Nothing. Top and bottom would have been Nothing in Nothing. So, Zero would have been Present. Zero would have been going on. If Zero is added with Zero, Zero is deducted from Zero, Zero is multiplied by Zero or Zero is divided by Zero, answer would have been Zero. Zero would have been as Many zeros among them a zero would have been same zero. A zero and Another zero would have been going on as Zero. Zero and Nothing would have been Zero. As Positive Nothing would have been containing the cause. As Zero, Nothing would have been positive. As Nothing, zero would have been negative. But positive Zero would have been going on as Zero containing meaning of Nothing. And Negative Nothing would have been going on containing the cause. As negative Zero would have been going on meaning of cause. Hence, as Nothing, Zero would have been believing that the cause is let enabled do have some and do any, those, who would have been graced, maybe regain themselves as Zero who wouldn't be lost whenever 'Zero' is either added, deducted, multiplied and divided by 'Zero' as Zero would be there to be many zeros who would be only all of each and every 'Zero'. Hence, for all Zeros, zero would go on as "I" and would do as,

"I" had done 'will' for You, "I" had believed, who might know
All of You, who had been striving or struggling,
Had not achieved what You had not known exactly.
But You had done what You could without having vehement belief.

"I" did 'will' for You, "I" again believed, who might know
All of You, who were exerting yourselves grappling,
Did not gain what You did not perceive definitely.
But You did what You could without having ardent belief.

"I" do 'will' for You, I still believe, who may know
All of You, who are making every effort or fighting,
May not bring about what You do not fathom out veraciously.
But You do what You can without having fervent belief.

"I" will do 'will' for You, "I" continue to believe, who perchance know

All of You, who will have been endeavouring or doing Your utmost,

Might have obtained what if You experience the belief literally.

But You will have to learn "I" do 'Will' only but not actually believe."

Notes

1) According to Indian spiritualistic literature there are five elements. They are Water, Orb, Room, Light, Draught.

i) Water = Water.

ii) Orb = One of the stars as well as one of the globe other than star.

iii) Room = Space.

iv) Light = Light.

v) Draught = Air.

2) Indweller = Who (The Atman i.e. Soul) indwells in body.

3) The Only "I" = The Almighty.

My Published books in English

1. I (published twice)
2. Self (published twice)
3. The State (a long poem)
4. What is Beyond! (poems)
5. The Sport (a long poem)
6. ?AND! (poems)
7. Nothing from Nothing (poems)
8. "S'HE'" (poems)
9. Obligation (stories)
10. Vivekananda (drama)
11. The Being (a long poem)
12. HE'art' (poems)
13. There 'i' am (poems)
14. KARANAGAMAHA (translation from Sanskrit to English)
15. ? (poems)

Published in Telugu

1. Kayakame Kailasam (novel-published twice)
2. Jnanasthalam (essays)
3. Akkamahadevi-Sadhana-Sandesham (essay)
4. Aadi Jagadguru Renukacharya (essay)
5. Sahavasi (stories)
6. Bejja MahaDevi (drama)
7. Kanuvippu (essays)
8. Sahavasi (stories)
9. Basaveshawara (drama)
10. Akshrabhyasam (essay)
11. Dampatyam (essay)
12. Kalyanam (essay)
13. Trinetra (poems)

14. Swatantriya Poratam 1857(Translation into Telugu from English)
15. Ramalambana (novel)
16. Jangam (poems)
17. Paarwateeshwara (poems)
18. Ishtalinga Puja (poems)
19. Anubhuti (poems)
20. Sadacharam (novel)
21. Bhajana (essay)